Maggie's Run

Maggie's Run

An Outback Brides Romance

Kelly Hunter

TULE
PUBLISHING

Maggie's Run
Copyright© 2018 Kelly Hunter
Tule Publishing First Printing, June 2018

The Tule Publishing Group, LLC

ALL RIGHTS RESERVED

First Publication by Tule Publishing Group 2018

No part of this book may be used or reproduced in any manner whatsoever without written permission except in the case of brief quotations embodied in critical articles and reviews.

This is a work of fiction. Names, characters, places, and incidents are products of the author's imagination or are used fictitiously. Any resemblance to actual events, locales, organizations, or persons, living or dead, is entirely coincidental.

ISBN: 978-1-949068-63-4

Please note the use of Australian English spelling and grammar throughout this story.

Chapter One

MAGGIE WALKER OFTEN wished she looked more intimidating. She could have taken after her late father, who'd been broad of shoulder, firm of jaw, and had cut an imposing figure no matter whose company he'd sought. She could have taken after her recently deceased great aunt, who'd been a model in her younger years—one of those aloof, impossibly leggy, aristocratic types. She could have been in possession of glacier-cut cheekbones, a piercing blue glare and enough height to make looking down on other people far too easy.

Maggie had inherited none of it.

Instead she'd topped out at five feet two, was slight of form and had a sweetness of face more commonly associated with wet kittens and baby fawns.

Intimidating she was not, but she'd rarely felt quite as invisible as she did now, standing in the main room of a sleepy country town's local stock and station agent, waiting for the guy behind the counter and currently on the phone to look her way. Maggie had spent her formative years in boarding school and was used to waiting her turn.

It had been quite a few years since anyone had tried to

pretend she wasn't there at all.

Florid of face and with a vocabulary that relied heavily on the word 'mate', the guy at the counter continued to ignore her. The shop front was clean, even if currently understaffed. It looked well stocked with supplies, as if they did good business. Hard to believe they did any business at all given their current attention to customer service.

Even a quick nod of acknowledgement would do.

The white farm truck she'd borrowed—no, not borrowed, it was hers now—had Wirra Station written on it in bold, black letters. Given that Maggie inheriting the historic sheep station had been the talk of Wirralong for going on two weeks now, and given that the vehicle could be clearly seen through the window, she was fairly sure *Mr I'm A Very Busy Man* knew who she was.

She took off her wide-brimmed hat and set it on the counter as she listened to him wax informative about feed ratios for racehorses. She took off her sunglasses and placed them on top of the hat. She kept her satchel full of paperwork slung over a too-narrow shoulder as she moseyed over towards a row of open office doors, but there was no-one inside any of the rooms. There was an exit through to the feed and fencing sheds out the back and a large red ship's bell hung beside the exit. Surely that was an invitation? She reached for the rope and rang it once, and then several times more because, frankly, she liked the sound of it.

The guy behind the counter paused mid-conversation to glare at her, and that was all the opening she needed. She'd been standing there for the past ten minutes, after all.

"I'm looking for James Henderson Junior," she said.

"He's not in today."

"That's a shame. Does he have a contact number that's not disconnected?"

"Look, lady, if James wants to stay in touch with a woman, he does."

"Good to know," she said politely. "What a champ." Maybe the guy behind the counter *hadn't* noticed the Wirra Station vehicle parked out front after all. "Thing is, I have here Carmel Walker's records of a dozen or so payments made to James these past six months for the installation of over sixty kilometres of rural fencing. And call me a city girl, but I've been over Wirra Station from top to bottom this past week and I can't find any new fences at all."

The guy gave up on his phone conversation with a muttered, "I'll call you back".

She headed back towards the counter, maintaining eye contact. No need to telegraph that her picture-perfect confidence stopped at the first layer of skin. "I'm Maggie Walker. I own Wirra Station now," she stated simply and didn't offer her hand.

"Kyle Henderson."

"Morning, Kyle." She looked around the store. "Family business, is it? James is your … brother? Father?" She'd never laid eyes on James but Kyle looked to be in his thirties, possibly a little younger.

"James is my cousin and, like I said, he's not here."

"Is there anyone else who can help me with my fencing query?"

"You said you had receipts," he countered flatly.

She pulled a sheaf of copies from her satchel and handed them to him. He flicked through them and frowned. "We haven't done any work for Wirra Station lately."

"I'm glad we agree. Am I in the right place? That's your letterhead? James Henderson's signature on the order form?"

He scowled, and she took it for a yes.

"So I'm in the right place." She leaned forward, palms on the counter, and fixed him with her most limpid gaze—the one he hadn't yet learned to be afraid of. "Sixty-eight kilometres of fencing at six thousand two hundred dollars a kilometre, installed. That's four hundred and twenty-one thousand six hundred dollars gone from Wirra Station's holding account. For fencing I can't find. That's a lot of fraud."

"Now look here, you crazy b—"

"Problems?" The deep voice that came from the doorway was instantly recognisable. The lazy drawl, the chocolate-coated rumble. The owner of that delectable voice was often at odds with her, or she with him, but he was never one to roar. Nor had she ever seen him back down. Not from a black snake in her great aunt's garden when they were kids, not from the wild dogs that had trapped her in the hay shed when she was ten. Not even from the hideous car accident that had cost her parents their lives.

Twelve-year-old Maxwell O'Connor had been the first

one to reach the accident scene all those years ago. Max had saved *her* and not them, and in the darkest corners of her heart she still hadn't forgiven him for that.

Maggie turned to face him reluctantly, wincing only slightly as she met his deep blue gaze. Warmer than the ocean, a couple of stars lighter than the midnight sky, his eyes were his best feature—assuming one discounted his voice. One also had to ignore his untamed mop of messy black hair, his country tan on a lean, rangy body and his smile. His smile was lethal. Good thing she so rarely saw it.

He had long legs and an excellent arse. She'd noticed both this morning as he'd sauntered away from her.

"Maxwell," she murmured warily.

"Margaret." Max's narrowed gaze flicked from her to the man behind the counter and then back to her again. "What's going on?"

"I was thinking about what you said this morning about Wirra Station's lack of decent fences." They'd had that particular conversation just after dawn, with her on one side of a tumbledown, two-strand wire fence and him on the other. His sheep had been on her land again. According to him, he'd had a gentleman's agreement with her great aunt that until the fences were fixed his sheep could go wherever they damn well pleased. "I remembered seeing a recent invoice for fencing amongst some paperwork, so I went back through Carmel's financial records and things just didn't add up. I popped in here to see where Wirra Station's sixty-eight kilometres of fully installed, fully paid for, rabbit-proof fencing was."

Maxwell spared her a flat glance, before turning towards Kyle.

"Max, you *know* I run the feed side of things," Kyle offered defensively. "The old man controls stock transport. Fencing and farm equipment is James's gig."

"Sadly, James isn't in," Maggie murmured. "Where exactly is James?"

"Ireland."

"And are you expecting him back any time soon, or has my dead aunt's money gone with him?"

"Maggie," Max barked. "Not helping."

"Oh, you have another approach?"

"Yeah, it's called holding your fire until you're damn sure you have the right people lined up."

She rather thought she had *exactly* the right people lined up and wondered whose word would prevail if negotiations turned ugly. She wasn't the local here, even if she could trace her lineage back to English settlement. "Fine." Her gaze clashed with Max's—heaven only knew what had him so riled—and then she turned back to the man behind the counter and summoned infinite patience and a smile.

"Kyle, let's start again. I have an accounts dispute with …" She glanced at the letterhead on the copied receipts. "… *Henderson's Stock and Station Agents* and I'd like to speak to someone who can answer my questions. Today. Otherwise my next step, *today,* will involve calling a lawyer. My father practised law back in Melbourne—it's probably not common knowledge around here anymore, but he did. Good schools. That Old Boys' network is alive and well—don't get me started. He was only in the early stages of his career when he died, but you wouldn't believe how successful some of his business partners are now. Barristers, lawmakers, Queen's Counsel. They still send me Christmas cards, I go to their children's weddings. They can be ridiculously protective of me and I am *absolutely* open to taking advantage of their expertise. So I'll ask again: Is there anyone here I can talk to about those missing fences?"

"You call that holding your fire?" Max was using his ever-so-patient drawl on her again. The one that never failed to wind her up.

"Why, yes, Max, I do. Do you hear me yelling? No. This is my *I know there must be a simple explanation around here somewhere* voice. Dulcet, isn't it?"

Max ignored her in favour of communicating with Kyle. "Sounds like Maggie needs to speak to the old man."

Kyle cleared his throat and said, "Let me make a call".

Maggie watched Kyle retreat into the very end office and shut the door before turning to Max once more and, honestly, could he not do something with his hair? Like tame it? Buy a comb? Hide it under a hat? Because just looking at it was making her fingers itch. "Is there a hairdresser in town?"

"What?"

"Because *there's* an appointment you don't want to miss."

"You're angry I stepped in to help." For someone who barely knew her, he had an uncanny knack for reading her thoughts.

"You *took over*. You always do. And I don't want or need you to."

Something that looked a lot like despair flashed across his face, and then the shutters came down and his expression hardened. "I don't always take over. For you, I've often held back."

Lucky her. "Did you know Carmel had ordered new fencing?"

"She mentioned it on occasion but in all honesty I never took much notice. I thought her fence talk was a delusion, the product of a tired mind. You weren't here once the dementia set in, Maggie. You didn't see the end." He grimaced and ran his hand through his hair and her fingers itched again. "I don't like the thought of anyone taking advantage of her on my watch."

"It wasn't your watch." Not even his overdeveloped sense of responsibility could make it so. "It was my watch, and I know full well I didn't do enough." She'd tried to get Carmel to leave Wirra Station, but Carmel hadn't budged.

"You could have come home."

Max was watching her closely, and Maggie drew herself up to her full height and tried to make like a willow. Someone who would bend but not break. "I had a home. One I'd made for myself." She'd also had a lover who'd been everything she'd ever wanted—right up until she hadn't been able to give him everything *he* wanted. "I *had* a life and it wasn't here." She couldn't hold Max's bright blue gaze any longer.

"I *know*, all right? I should have come back years ago to care for the woman who'd been forced to take care of me. That's how debts are paid. But I didn't, and that's a matter for me and my conscience and approximately no-one else."

Silence met her speech and she risked a quick glance in his direction. He'd broadened his stance, shoved his hands in the pockets of his jeans. Not for him the shiny boots and spotless country wear of the stock and station agent. He was dressed for work and dirty with it. Mud on his boots and a slash of something greasy along his forearm.

"Sorry," she muttered. "I'm already feeling guilty about being the too-little-too-late girl." She was also feeling ever so slightly overwhelmed by the responsibility of caring for Wirra Station, not to mention unexpectedly weepy over the loss of a woman she'd never seen eye to eye with. "Doesn't mean people can cheat a dying old lady and no-one's going to care. Doesn't mean I don't want what's best for Wirra Station."

He studied her as if she were a bug beneath a microscope. He always had been able to make her feel far smaller than she already was.

"Care to discuss that admirable sentiment over lunch? I might have a proposal or two to put to you."

"You want to sell Wirra Station some non-existent fencing too?"

She'd gone too far. She didn't need his stony glare to tell her that.

"Sorry," she muttered. "No excuses, just ... sorry."

Again.

"Why do you always get so defensive around me?" How such a sexy rumble of a voice could sound so tightly controlled and full of authority she didn't know. "I'd like to take you to lunch and discuss Wirra Station with you. I'd like to help you with your fencing questions because if James *has* been paid for services not rendered I'm going to feel somewhat responsible for not picking up on that. Lunch—yes or no? My thoughts on fencing options—yes or no?"

"I—yes." There was an argument on her tongue but she swallowed it down. *You and Max fight over the colour of the sky.* Carmel's words coming back to haunt her. But then there was the snake that hadn't bitten her because of him, and the dogs that hadn't savaged her because of him, and that time she'd been drenching sheep in the sun all day and running a scorching temperature by the end of it, and he'd dumped her in a water trough and kept her there and cursed a blue streak at his stupidity and hers. There was care in there somewhere, rough and ready, but it was there. She was alive because of him.

Like it or not, Maxwell O'Connor's assistance was worth something.

"Yes to both," she offered with all the politeness she'd ever been taught. "Thank you."

He eyed her warily. "That was almost too easy."

"Yeah, well. I'm feeling nostalgic. I'm sure it'll pass."

There was that smile again, just a hint of it, and she looked away quickly before it did things to her libido. Like remind her she had one.

Kyle returned and his glance encompassed them both. "The old man—James Senior—he's still at the sale yards. Says he'll be back by two but it's going to take longer than that to pull our financials and get hold of James Junior. If you could give us the rest of today, we'll give you a call first thing tomorrow. The old man wants you to know that if there's a problem at our end we'll fix it."

Max said nothing. Maggie slipped her sunnies on and picked up her hat. "Fix it how?"

"Lady … Ms. Walker—" Kyle the no-longer-cocky paused and shook his head. "—The old man's the best one to talk to from here on in. If James has pulled a fast one—and I'm not saying he has—then he's a moron. He'll be finished in this town and within the family. I don't know what kind of fix we'll be offering, but Henderson's will see you right. The Henderson *family* will see you right."

She glanced towards Max and he gave the slightest nod. She hadn't been looking to take her cue from him. Or maybe she had and she just didn't want to admit it. "Thanks, Kyle." She thought back to his earlier phone call for something pleasant to say. "Good luck with feeding those racehorses."

And Kyle arced up again. "Is that a threat?"

Now she was coming across as intimidating? How could he possibly have interpreted her parting words in that fashion? "Actually, I was aiming for vaguely friendly, but …" She gave an awkward wave of her hand. "I get the impression I missed that particular mark altogether. It happens."

Was that a snort from Max? She thought it was and told herself she didn't care if he was laughing at her abysmal people skills. Not everyone could be country friendly and utterly at ease with themselves and the world in general.

Head high and chin up, Maggie started for the door and somehow Max was there to open it for her, his manners ingrained in the same way his saviour complex was built into the fabric of his bones. He was who he was and so be it. Confidence was sexy. Old-fashioned manners were sexy too.

Who knew?

"Thank you," she muttered, and there was an echo of another older thank you woven in there somewhere. A thank you she could barely bring herself to remember, such was her shame at how unwillingly she'd once offered it.

"You're welcome."

MAX FOLLOWED MAGGIE in his truck, careful not to rush her as she parked out front of the Wirralong pub. He pulled up a couple of empty parking spots away, careful not to crowd her, because Maggie never had done anything but attack when pressured. He'd come into town for a stop valve and ended up taking Maggie Walker to lunch, but he wasn't complaining. He had plenty to say to her—assuming they could sit and eat together peacefully.

They were older and wiser than they'd once been.

A man could hope.

He hadn't liked the situation he'd walked in on at Henderson's. Old Jim Henderson was as solid as they came, but Kyle had a mean streak and James Junior was a Casanova and a gambler both. Damn right she'd be dealing with the elder Henderson from now on in. He'd make sure of it.

It didn't help that she was still pocket sized and more beautiful than a person had any right to be. Scramble a man's brain just by looking at her. She'd always scrambled his. Too stubborn for her own good. Never asked for help, even if she needed it. Especially if she needed it. He could still remember the feel of her slight form; wet, bedraggled and burning up against him after a day spent drenching sheep. She'd fought against him, even in the throes of heatstroke. He'd never been so furious at both her and himself for not calling an early halt to the stinking hot workday. She'd been the bane of his existence that summer, every too-stubborn, too-fragile inch of her.

He'd taken Maggie back to his place and watched as his mother had made her drink water and tended her until her core temperature had dropped to within reason and then put her to bed. He'd sat down to dinner amidst silent recrimination for working Maggie so hard, and he'd eaten what he could and then excused himself outside to throw up every last bit of it.

His father had found him later, shivering but not from cold, and had sat there with him in silence, tendering no judgement, no words at all, until much, much later when he'd said he figured Max had probably caught some heatstroke too and did he want to come back inside. The little Walker chit was awake and getting skittish. Fierce as a wet kitten, his father had said, but otherwise okay and looking for something familiar to fix on.

That something familiar being him.

Years before that he'd held Maggie in his arms and watched the blood leak out of her belly as her family car had fireballed in front of them. She'd fought him that time too, kicking and screaming to be free of him and he'd held on so tight. Held on, because if he hadn't he'd have lost her.

He'd been twelve to her eleven and they'd called him a hero for pulling Maggie from the wreckage. Everyone but Maggie had called him a hero and her stilted thank you had been forcibly given. He'd *heard* the crack of Carmel's hand as she'd ordered Maggie into Wirra Station's formal sitting room to thank him for her life. He'd seen the handprint on Maggie's face as she'd faced him and said the words demanded of her. He'd sat there in that stuffy old room, scrubbed clean and dressed in his Sunday best, and for the first time in his life he hadn't known what was expected of him. He'd been supposed to ask Maggie how she was, but her parents were dead and her great-aunt could barely stand the sight of her, so he'd sat there in silence instead of saying something stupid.

He'd done a lot of that over the years—especially around this woman.

The front bar of the Wirralong pub was largely empty at this time of day but the brasserie out back had a good number of customers for a town with just over five thousand people, and more to the point, it was air conditioned.

"What are your plans for Wirra Station?" he asked, when they'd put their food orders in and he'd set a cold lime soda on the coaster in front of her.

"I don't know yet."

"Because if you're looking to sell, I'm looking to buy."

She raised a delicate eyebrow as if he'd surprised her. "Can you afford it?"

"Yes."

"Which of your operations are you looking to expand?"

"Fat cows, fine wool merinos and some feed cropping."

"What if you just took grazing rights and leased the land from me?"

But he'd already considered that idea and discarded it. "There's too much infrastructure work to be done. Fencing, water, weed control. Sowing new pasture and getting it established. The land's not fit for use as is and I'm not willing to put the work in if I only benefit for a couple of years."

"I see." She studied her hands, so slender and fine. Her nails were short but shapely. He wanted to reach out and run his fingertips across her knuckles to see if her skin was as soft as it looked. He had a feeling her skin would always feel soft to his work-roughened hands. He looked up to find her studying him, her expression defeated and somehow sad. "Well, then. I guess it's yours if you want it."

It was almost too easy. "No-one you need to run that

decision by?"

"I'm the last Walker standing." Her smile turned jagged. "The decision's all mine."

And still it felt forced upon her. "You could keep it. Stay and run it."

Fight for it.

"Nah," she offered quietly. "Carmel wasn't one for teaching, and I know next to nothing about running a farming operation the way it should be run."

As far as he could tell, Carmel hadn't known much about that either. "You could learn." But she was already shaking her head.

"I don't want to learn. My memories of the place aren't the best and there's no money left in the Wirra Station accounts, just debt and plenty of it. I'd have to sell the Melbourne house I inherited from my parents in order to make the kind of improvements the place needs to become functional again. Weed control, sowing pastures, buying stock…" She shook her head. "There are three hundred head of sheep left on the books, not that I can find them, and apparently you're looking after some Wirra Station rams. Artificial insemination. Quarterly cheques from you. There's been no other income for the past two years."

It was worse than he thought. "Those three hundred sheep you're missing are running with my mob now. They're the last of Wirra Station's breeding stock and they're worth more than you know. Carmel would never sell them to me outright but she did let me run them. Between her bloodlines and mine, we're producing the best fine wool merino fleeces in the state. There should be a wool cheque or two from me in your accounts as well." He'd known Carmel was running lean. He'd been generous. "I know they've been cashed."

"I'll take another look," she murmured. "The accounts are a mess. I put in a couple of hours a day on them and it's all I can do not to tear my hair out."

She had beautiful hair. Fine light brown that caught the sun and ribboned towards gold. "You should keep the hair," he offered and won a tiny smile from her.

"It's not just the hair. And it's not that I'm madly attached to the Melbourne house and would never sell it. It's stuffed full of dead people too, just like Wirra Station, but it doesn't demand everything Wirra Station does, you know? Work wise. Nightmare wise."

"What kind of nightmares?"

She said nothing. Wouldn't even look at him.

"Because just for the record, I still wake up screaming about fire and ash and red dust and death." She looked at him in shock and he tried to paper over the great gaping hole he'd ripped in his defences. "Not always. Just sometimes," he muttered. "That night was formative."

They'd never talked about it, not once. He'd never known how to begin. Given Maggie's silence, probably not like this.

The food came and he dug in, even though he'd never felt less like eating.

They sat there while Maggie pushed her meal around her plate and the property deal of a lifetime hovered over him like a stain. He didn't want to blow the deal. Wirra Station had been neglected for far too long and needed someone who knew the lay of the land to take it in hand. Someone who could make the most of it, namely him.

But he'd cut off his right arm before doing wrong by Maggie Walker ever again.

"You could marry me," he offered quietly, and in all honesty, he wasn't quite sure where that had come from.

She blinked. Opened her mouth as if to protest and closed it again on nothing but air.

He ploughed on, trying to make sense of his own thoughts on the matter. Most of which revolved around him being there for her and holding her in his arms when the nightmares started up again, although how *that* could ever do anything other than trap them inside that fatal night was anyone's guess. And still he ploughed on. Possibly the farmer in him. "You contribute the land, I bring the infrastructure money and management expertise. O'Connor Enterprises expands. Wirra Station comes to life again. You also get to keep your Melbourne house, so you can head off for a city fix whenever the isolation becomes too much. Everybody wins."

Her eyes widened but her mouth stayed firmly shut. The limb he was stretched out on felt way too lean to hold the weight of his offer.

"It's a business opportunity, Maggie. People marry for reasons other than love all the time."

"Yes, but—" She waved a slender hand in his direction. "Don't you want to marry someone who likes you? Or even loves you? Because that really doesn't seem like too big an ask." She did that hand waving thing again. "For you. I mean, you come from one of those families who support each other. Your parents love each other. Why would you settle for less?"

Good question.

He watched as she subsided into silence and reached for her lime soda. He waited. He was good at waiting.

"You must want Wirra Station a lot," she said at last.

He did. He also thought she was underestimating the hold she'd always had on him. A lot. "Just a thought."

"I'm not marrying you," she said flatly, and the strength of his disappointment took him by surprise.

"Fair enough. I'm aware it was a long shot." Hadn't stopped him from taking it though. She eyed him warily and if there was any defence against shuttered doe eyes and ridiculously long black lashes, he hadn't yet found it. "Although I do still think we'd be compatible."

"*Compatible?*" She sounded incredulous. "The first time I met you, I was five and visiting with my parents and you and your father were out in Carmel's woolshed with a pregnant ewe. You had your skinny six-year-old hand and half your arm all up inside the animal. They'd fetched you from school because your hand was small enough to fit and you were cheaper than a vet."

He shook his head at the memory and tried to suppress a

grin. "The look on your face."

"You were six! Who does that to a six-year-old?"

"Yeah, but the ewe lived and the lambs lived and I got to wash my hands and eat cake and miss school."

"See? This is what I mean. We are not compatible. I am *not* cut out to be a farming person."

"If it helps any, these days I'd probably just ring the vet. Even if I did have a six-year-old handy."

"And then there's the not-so-small matter of children." She made it sound like an accusation. "I'm assuming you want them eventually, if not sooner."

"Yes." Why lie?

"A business union won't get you children."

"No? Because it might."

"Not with me it won't."

She sounded all the way certain and the expression on her face warned him not to push his luck. They were still talking. Negotiating. She hadn't started cursing him. Yet. "Tell me something, Margaret Mary, and be honest. Are all your thoughts of Wirra Station bad ones? Do you have any love for the homestead and the land at all?"

"Why? Are the town folk worried I'm going to sell off a piece of their history to a soulless overseas conglomerate?"

As far as he was concerned, the people of Wirralong were a pragmatic lot. "As long as whoever buys it runs it as it should be run—stocks it and looks after it and creates jobs—I doubt anyone's going to care who owns it."

Her mouth curled. "You'd care."

"Yes, I would." No point denying it. "I want it to be me."

"So do I." She squared her shoulders as if preparing for battle. "You say you can afford it. Make an offer, a reasonable market-value offer, and it's yours."

"I have one condition."

She eyed him warily.

"I want you to stay on for three months, full time, to sort through everything in the homestead while I act as your farm manager and get the land ready for use. I can teach you everything you need to know about running the place and if you still want to go ahead with the sale after that, I'm all for it. We factor the money I've already spent on improvements into the sale price. You'll walk away a rich woman without a care in the world. Life of luxury. *But ...* if at the end of the three months you decide to stay on, you sell your Melbourne house, pay me back what I've spent, and the place is yours to run, and run well, from that point onwards."

She sat back in her chair and studied him as if he were some fascinating new creature that might bite if she ventured any closer. "Why would you do that for me? Is this some kind of 'you saved my life and now you're responsible for me forever more' thing?"

"No, this is me thinking that with Carmel gone and no-one around to judge you and find you wanting, you might be able to see past the nightmares and begin to appreciate your heritage."

"Why do you care?"

"Because I do." He'd had enough of this conversation. "Before I buy the place—and God knows I want to... Before I claim what's yours I need you to know and fully understand what you're giving up."

He stood. Time to leave before he started offering her various essential body parts currently in his possession. "If Henderson wants to do the work you've already paid for, you might want to mention a few other services you're in need of. A new dam at the bottom of the south ridge. Water troughs, tanks, pipes and seals, pumps."

"You want me to buy *more* from them?" She sounded confused rather than incredulous.

"Didn't say anything about buying it. They've had your money for quite some time. Charge interest and take it out in trade. Call it a warning for anyone with a mind to scam the new owner of Wirra Station. Word'll get around soon enough. It's what I'd do."

"Yeah, but I'm not sure what you do is always wise."

She would know.

She was still looking at him as if she'd never seen him before and he'd had enough of it. He'd been bound to her in tragedy and death since he was twelve years old. He knew the shape of her screams and she knew the sting of his tears. She *knew* him, for better and for worse. "Are we drawing up this contract of sale or not?"

"I'm thinking about it."

Nothing stopping her from selling the place to someone who wouldn't saddle her with unwanted terms and conditions. Nothing but a shared history neither of them wanted to recall.

"What are you going to do if I don't accept your terms and conditions?" she asked.

"Move on." Property acquisition of a lifetime and he'd blown it. He nodded, and headed for the door, not wanting her to see how much he cared. He really should have known better than to get his hopes up.

Dealing with Maggie Walker had always cost more than he could afford.

Chapter Two

MAGGIE WATCHED MAXWELL O'Connor swagger out the door of the dining room and only realised she'd been staring once he'd gone. Moments later a waitress came to clear the table.

"I see you've met the O'Connor," the woman said with an Irish lilt of her own.

"*The* O'Connor?"

"Well, he does have parents, but believe me when I say there's only one of him." The girl smiled and her dark eyes smiled with her. It seemed impossible not to smile back.

"He drives me nuts," she offered reluctantly, and the other woman laughed.

"Can I get you anything else?"

"No thanks, I'm done." The name tag said the woman's name was Maeve.

"So … you're new around here? I've not seen you before," said Maeve.

Maggie hesitated, and then cursed her instinctive reserve. Standoffishness didn't go down well in Wirralong. She'd learned that lesson the hard way. "I've just inherited Wirra Station. I'm the only Walker left, so here I am."

"Oh, so you're the one." Maeve made it sound like an honour. "The whole town's talking about you."

"I know." She stood up. "Thanks for the meal. It was good."

"We do an even better Sunday roast."

"I'll keep that in mind."

Maggie was through the front door and out on the wide, verandah covered pavement moments later. The pub stood at one end of Wirralong's main drag, which consisted of two blocks worth of shops and services, some of which were hanging on by a thread. There'd been money here a hundred years ago, and plenty of it, but the days of the golden fleece were long gone. Like many small country towns with declining populations, Wirralong struggled to survive.

Why she'd once been so daunted by the simple act of walking down the main street of the town was anyone's guess. Maybe it was because the people in it had never failed to make her feel small and mean and petty for being reserved around strangers. Stuck up. Unfriendly. Words she'd been labelled with back when she'd been newly orphaned and terrified of her own shadow. A judgement she'd never been able to overthrow.

Several years of therapy and behaviour modification strategies later, she could at least recognise how other people saw her, and try to counter it, even if she did still revert to aloof, stand-offish type when hard pressed.

All she had to do to make a better impression was have the confidence to believe that she was worth something.

Worth talking to, worth getting to know. Worth the effort.

Max had always thought she was worth the effort and still did, judging by his offer to teach her about farming and give her time to make up her mind about what she wanted to do.

She crossed the road, deep in thought and wanting to walk off the meal she mostly hadn't eaten by doing a lap of the main street. Memories and a glimpse of glorious red hair through a shopfront window caused her to stop and smile in recognition. She'd seen that same red hue at the funeral, taken condolences and weathered a hug and a promise to catch up, but she hadn't done anything about it so far. She could start here when it came to digging back into the fabric of the town. She could be friendly and accessible. Fake it 'til you make it.

The sign said *Hair Affair*. The redhead looked up, her bright eyes and ready smile radiating a warm welcome. Elsa O'Donoghue was one of those rare people who'd always had a smile for Maggie, no matter how awkward Maggie had been. Elsa waved her in and Maggie went.

"Hey," she said as she stepped inside, only to be engulfed in a warm hug and a cloud of curly red hair.

"Finally," said Elsa. "I thought Wirra Station had swallowed you whole."

"It still might." Maggie returned the hug and the smile and extricated herself gently. It wasn't that she didn't like touch—it was more that she never quite knew how to respond to it. She looked around the salon. It had a row of mirrors and hair-cutting stations, a couple of washing and rinsing hair basins and a small front counter with a row of hair products behind it. Nothing flash, but it was clean, bright and cheerful—a pure reflection of its proprietor. A client was sipping something that looked like green tea and half-heartedly reading a magazine while waiting for the goop on her hair to do whatever that particular goop did. Music played cheerfully in the background, something surprisingly *not* country or western or both. "So this is the booming business?"

"It is." Elsa spread her arms wide. "I'm starting small and working my way towards greatness. You like?"

"I love it. I bet you get customers coming in and wanting their hair exactly the same as yours."

"Are you kidding? This hair of mine takes work, not to mention it's red. And I have freckles."

"You don't have that many freckles." Maggie gestured towards Elsa's nose. They'd had this conversation before and there was comfort in it. "That there's a smattering of freckles."

Elsa reached out to test the length of the bangs that framed Maggie's face. "Now that's a good cut," she murmured. "Frames your face to perfection. Where'd you get it done?"

"Melbourne."

"Figures. Any time you want it done better, you just give me a call."

"Oooh, big talk and confidence. I like that."

"And it won't cost you the earth," said the woman in the chair.

"Better book me in for next week, then," said Maggie and watched Elsa do just that.

"So you're staying?" asked Elsa. "Because pretty much the whole town wants to know."

"I don't know what I'm doing yet. Did you know that Wirra Station used to breed racehorses once?"

"No, but it would explain the size of the stables," said Elsa. "Is there any burning reason why you have to go back to Melbourne to live?"

"Not a one. That's as far as I've got on the what to do with Wirra Station front. Having said that, if I stay on much longer I'm going to need a plumber. I need a new hot water system and a new shower head. Decent water pressure. In my wilder dreams I install a whole new shower recess."

"Is it that bad?"

"Worse. The 1920s was not a luxurious time for bathrooms." And given that there'd been no major renovations since then, the homestead was authentic in the extreme. "I'm praying I can get at least some things fixed without running afoul of the heritage listing on the place."

"You should be able to modernise the wet rooms, provided you keep the exterior as is," said the woman in the chair, giving up all pretence of not listening. "Jeannie Lamb. My husband's a builder. He doesn't do bathrooms, but he can recommend someone who will, and he has a lot of experience with heritage home repairs. We don't call them renovations, by the way, and the first thing he'll tell you is that it's better to go in hard with a fully visualised restoration plan rather than constantly putting forward piecemeal changes. Even if it takes you years to get things done, get the permissions out of the way fast. Trust me, getting heritage foundation permission to make changes is something you only want to do once."

"There you go," said Elsa. "Words from the wise. Jeannie, this is Maggie Walker. Maggie just inherited Wirra Station. Jeannie and her husband bought the Burke place a few years back in a fit of enthusiasm for simple country living."

"And ignorance," added Jeannie. "Don't forget the ignorance. Bottom line is my Ron's a builder and I trained as an architect too many years ago to count. We're both retired, but Ron stays busy doing the odd job here and there and I still have my contact list and can source anything you want by way of building materials and furnishings."

"I do like the sound of that." It was talent Maggie hadn't expected to find here. "Where is the Burke place again?"

"Out past the old school ruin," said Elsa.

"Ah."

"You have no idea where I'm talking about, do you?" asked Elsa, laughing.

"Absolutely none. But I do have another question for you."

Elsa nodded.

"Maxwell O'Connor."

Elsa's accompanying hum was downright appreciative.

"Not you too."

"Hey, I have eyes. And then there's his—"

Maggie held up her hand. "I don't need a list of the man's virtues." She had eyes too. "I want the gossip. What's he been doing since high school? Strengths. Weaknesses. Moneymaking ventures."

Elsa's eyes had narrowed ever so slightly. "Why?"

"Because I'm curious."

"Curious as in wildly attracted to him, or curious as in you want to ruin the man?"

"Curious in that he wants to buy Wirra Station and I want to know where the money's coming from."

"Oh. That's an easy one." Elsa was back to her sunny self. "Max took off around the world after school on an agricultural exchange. One of those a few months here, a few months there, a few months everywhere kind of deals. He ended up staying away for four or five years and setting up an international wool co-op that auctions superfine wool directly to high-end Italian and Chinese processors. The wool's the best of the best. By the time he rolled back into Wirralong he was a self-made man with an Italian model girlfriend."

"Oh." Well. "Good for him."

"The O'Connors bought the Camerons out a few years back and doubled the size of their operation. Makes sense he'd have his eye on Wirra Station too. Jewel in the crown."

Maggie snorted. "Clearly you haven't seen the place lately."

"She may be an old lady but she will always be majestic," said Elsa. "And if you think Max wouldn't take care of her, you're wrong. He's got a lot of time for what's his."

"Maybe I could sell him the land and use the money to do up the house and the outbuildings." An idea was starting to form, one that didn't involve a new career as a farmer, or playing by Maxwell O'Connor's rules. "I could turn it into a bed and breakfast. Or a function centre that specialises in woolshed weddings." Wirra Station had a monstrous woolshed. It too was heritage listed. "Or garden weddings." Mustn't forget the garden. No-one who'd seen it ever did.

"Now you're talking," said Elsa. "You could offer a complete wedding package. Married in the garden and the reception in the woolshed. Put the wedding party in the house beforehand and the newlyweds in the stockman's cabin afterwards. This idea's got legs."

This idea was nuts. "I'd need a builder." May as well embrace the full fantasy. "A team of builders, fully committed to the project."

"Hello-o?" Elsa pointed a hairbrush at Jeannie. "And I can think of at least three tradesmen in town who'd be one hundred per cent on board with committing to the kind of work you'd need done. Just think—eventually these high-society weddings are going to need caterers and waitstaff and florists and make-up artists. *Hairdressers.*" At this, the brush got pointed in Elsa's direction. "It's a brilliant idea."

"Why high-society weddings? Why not ordinary weddings?"

"Because high society is where you're socially connected. It's your thing."

"You're mistaking the orphan being sent to a posh boarding school with the orphan being *liked* at the posh boarding school," Maggie said.

"You *will* have to work on your people skills," said Elsa with a grin.

"Bite me. I'm *much* better than I was. Okay, slightly better. Okay, that's what employees are for." Maybe the aloof aristocrat was alive and well in her after all. But the idea of making something out of Wirra homestead was beginning to grow on her. Could she really turn that bag of bones and bad memories into something positive? A place where love was celebrated and good memories thrived? "I'm an unemployed art historian turned part-time photographer, not a … whatever that would make me."

"The word you're looking for is entrepreneur," said Elsa.

"I'd never get the money back that I'd be pouring into the place. It'd be a labour of love." And given that she really didn't love the place … "Possibly a labour of stupidity."

"And philanthropy," said Jeannie. "You'd be restoring a significant historical building and opening it up for public use. That's a public service."

Elsa nodded enthusiastically.

"I don't know," said Maggie. "Change isn't always welcome around here."

"You'd need to bring the townspeople on board with

your plan," said Jeannie airily, as if that was the easy part. "Start with fundraising woolshed dances for the Rural Fire Service, while the building work is still in progress. Let them see and experience what you're trying to create. Offer your woolshed and paddock space as a once-a-month venue where classic car enthusiasts can gather. You're going to need them onside so that they'll offer bridal vehicle services. Have a medical services fundraiser evening when you're ready to trial your catering team for the first time. Goodwill and publicity all rolled into one."

"Yes," said Elsa. "All of this."

"Whoa," said Maggie. "I'm a professional fundraiser now? Back up, way back, to the part where I need a plumber and a new hot water system."

"You know what else you need?" said Elsa. "Support for your vision."

"My wha—"

"We should start a ladies' night in. A time and place where we can dream big and spin ideas and pamper ourselves. We could have it here to begin with. First Monday or Tuesday of the month, how does that sound? I'm free. Make our skills all open and accessible. Jeannie, you in?"

"I'm possibly in," said Jeannie with the smiley age lines. "Got to pace myself."

"I'll ask Serenity—she's the beautician who works from the back of this place." Elsa was on an all-inclusive roll. "Green hair this month and a music playlist that not everyone can appreciate. You'll like her."

"I will?" Okay, no need to get all sceptical. "I mean, sure. Why wouldn't I?"

"I'm predicting you'll bond over your many failed attempts to make sense of other people. And she's the best make-up artist I've ever seen and you're going to need her once the bridal parties start arriving. I say get in early and secure her services."

"It would probably be pointless to remind you that this wedding business does not yet exist." Although it was worth a try, nonetheless.

"Pointless." Elsa nodded sagely. "I'll organise that ladies' night. Afternoon. Whatever. Friday. Five-thirty. See you then."

IT PROBABLY HADN'T been *The O'Connor's* influence that made James Henderson Senior so very compliant when he called to speak with Maggie the following morning. Two teams of fencers would work day in and day out until the fencing that had been paid for was done. There would be water troughs and tanks delivered and installed. Pipes, two windmills, three pumps, one dam and a hot water system he'd heard she was looking for, and someone who could install it—he threw it all her way at no extra cost and Maggie let him.

Max had said it wouldn't be wrong; that it would make her position strong in the eyes of others and such things would matter if she was staying on.

If she was staying on.

The dream she'd spun about turning the homestead into a destination wedding venue was refusing to let her go and the more time she spent opening up rooms that hadn't seen daylight or fresh air in years, the more it began to seem like a possibility. The homestead was a stunning piece of architecture, even in its old age. Eleven bedrooms, three drawing rooms, a formal dining room, a library, even a sizeable ballroom that opened onto a verandah that led directly to the garden. A garden that had *never* been neglected the way the rest of Wirra Station had been let go.

Generations of Walkers had thrived here once. And Maggie had a yearning, as the last of them, to make the house look loved and cared for and happy before she let it go.

If she let it go.

It was different without Carmel here. Less anxiousness on Maggie's part. No-one waiting to tell her not to poke and pry and stay out of this room and that room. She'd had to get Jeannie's Ron over simply to unlock the doors of some of the rooms. The keys were either long gone or still hidden, and it wasn't so much that she expected to find dead bodies or gruesome histories in those rooms that had been abandoned … but she was rather relieved when she didn't.

They were little time capsules of the lives of the people who once lived here, that was all, and she still didn't know what she was going to do with them.

The historian in her wanted to photograph and document everything before moving a thing.

If she had money to spend she'd get a team of people in to help her do it. So much could be done here, and quickly, if money was plentiful and vision ruled.

Maggie made coffee and took it out to the verandah, the wide wooden planks beneath her feet smooth and warm from a patch of morning sun. She sat with her back to a post and her face turned towards the hills and the faint outline of the Grampian Ranges to the west. The view was spectacular, as always, and the darting of honeyeaters in and out of the flowering salvias made her smile.

Of all the things Carmel had neglected in her later years, her garden hadn't been one of them. Five acres of beautifully tended and carefully watered vistas with ancient trees that soared and shrubbery that bloomed even in the harshest conditions. For as long as Maggie had known her, Carmel had paid gardener Bob Steele a regular working wage to make sure of it. He came four days a week, starting at six and finishing at three and he'd be in again tomorrow, because Maggie had yet to let him go. He kept to himself and liked plants more than people and she could see the question in his eyes every time he said good morning and goodbye.

Provision had been made for him in Carmel's will—the cottage he'd lived in as part of his wage package was his now, free and clear.

She didn't think it was financial security that was bothering him.

What of the garden and my role here? What are you going to do with my thirty years of toil and the living legacy I protect?

She wondered what Bob would think of her grand plans to hold weddings here. Most artists liked to show off their work.

Didn't they?

Halfway through her coffee, Maggie heard the sound of a vehicle approaching. By the time the truck rolled to a stop and Max got out, she was standing at the top of the verandah steps and raising a hand in greeting. Hard to say why the sight of him made her stand a little straighter and her heart beat a little faster, but it did. It always had.

"Whatever happened to your Italian model girlfriend?" she asked, without thinking.

He stopped at the bottom of the steps and eyed her warily. "And good morning to you too."

Ah. Yes. She smiled awkwardly and cursed her general lack of manners around this man. "Someone mentioned her in passing the other day. And seeing as you more or less suggested a business union—

"You mean when I asked you to marry me?"

"Yes. That. I wondered what became of her. Maybe she did you wrong and you're broken-hearted and can never love another, so a business union doesn't bother you, and ..." She faltered beneath his amused blue gaze. "What?"

"You're still chewing on my proposal. I like that."

Maggie gave his comment the snarl it deserved. "I'm not chewing. I spat it out. Now I'm looking at it with vague curiosity before I cover it with dirt."

"Classy."

Yeah, no. So much for her very expensive education in manners and deportment. Time to try and redeem herself. "Coffee?"

He nodded and headed with her towards the kitchen. West to the end of the verandah, turn, third door past the ballroom and wipe your boots before stepping inside. Not that Maggie was wearing boots. Her feet were bare but for satin silver nail polish on her toes.

"Saacha was never my girlfriend," he offered in that deep, dark rumble of his as he stepped through the door. "Her family owns fabric mills and she has a direct line to several fashion houses. We became business partners, successful ones, but never more than that. She married her childhood sweetheart and they have a four-year-old daughter called Maxxie, named after me because I was on hand to help deliver her when she arrived a month early. Saacha was grateful—once she stopped screaming. They visit every year and parade down the main street, with Saacha calling Maxxie by name every chance she gets. Mainly because Saacha's a stirrer and thinks it's hilarious that everyone around here thinks Maxxie's mine. My mother then spends the next six months setting everyone straight."

"Sounds like … fun?"

"They like it."

"And you?"

"Apparently it adds to my mystique."

"You have mystique?"

He reached for the coffee mugs in the cupboard beside his head. "These days I'm almost as mysterious as you."

"Me?"

"C'mon, Maggie. You disappear for years at a time and no-one knows where you are or what you're doing because you never keep in touch and Carmel was never one to say. You turn up again, the last of the Walkers, just in time to inherit an iconic sheep station. Mystique is your middle name."

"Do you still take your coffee strong and muddy?"

He eyed the gleaming red coffee machine on the counter. "That's new."

"It's my pride and joy and if you ask me nicely I'll make you any kind of coffee you want." Wouldn't hurt to butter him up. She was, after all, about to make him an offer he may well refuse. "What if I were to offer you a double-strength Italian espresso with warm milk on the side?" She could tell he was tempted. "Mmm?"

"Maggie, you're being friendly. This is not normal. You're up to something."

"This is true." No point denying it. "I've been thinking about what I might do with this place. I'd like to run a new option past you."

"Go ahead." His voice was carefully devoid of anything resembling emotion, but his body betrayed him, coiled tight and still.

"I'd like to know whether you'd be willing to buy the

farming land and let me keep the homestead and outbuildings, the woolshed and a couple of hundred acres around them all."

Surely it wasn't that bad an idea, but he was already shaking his head. "Carmel wanted to split Wirra Station in two and sell part of it off a few years back but she couldn't get permission to do so. The powers that be wouldn't let her split the title."

"Why not?"

"I assume it was because of the heritage listing. You could try again, see if anything has changed." His expression warned her not to hold her breath.

"I will."

"What were you thinking of doing with the homestead?" He'd relaxed a little. Not as rigidly still as before, but still wary. He was invested in the fate of Wirra Station and she liked him better for it. Elsa's words that he looked after what was his whispered through her mind, and Maggie was a believer. She'd never known otherwise from him. "And why the woolshed?"

"Ah. I had a cunning plan. Actually, I was going to ask if I could keep the drover's hut up in the foothills too."

"What for?"

"To put honeymooners in."

Max blinked. It had been a while since she'd rendered him speechless, and she took way too much pleasure in it.

"Excuse me?" he said finally.

"The honeymooners, who would have been getting married here on account of the wedding venue business I was going to create."

"So ... has this been a lifelong ambition of yours?"

"Not exactly." She fiddled around with the lid of the biscuit jar and tried to remember one ambition, just one, that Carmel hadn't criticised. Better to simply not have ambition to begin with. "But it might have been fun to try and be an entrepreneur, and you have to admit that the bones of such a business are already here. The woolshed, the gardens, eleven bedrooms, the ballroom ... If you could have bought the land, I'd have had enough money in my pocket to go all out and bring this place back to life. Maybe it would have been cathartic. Maybe by watching others find the beauty in this place, I might be able to see it too."

"Don't you see it already?"

"Sometimes I do. You were right about me feeling more welcome here now."

Now that Carmel had gone.

Max sighed heavily. Eyed her balefully. "Where's my coffee? I need coffee for this." He ran a heavy hand through his hair and she felt her hand twitch in response. It wasn't up to her to restore order to the mess he'd just made. He probably *liked* the shaggy glory of it. "It's not something you're going to be able to do overnight. Overcome sixty years of neglect. Set up a business while you're at it."

"No, it's not." He wasn't shutting the idea down outright, and she took hope from that.

"You'd need tradesmen, specialist restoration builders.

They're expensive, not to mention hard to lure all the way out here for a job."

"I have a couple of leads."

"Then there's the cost of continued maintenance once you've got it how you want it." His gaze skittered to the blackened stone behind the kitchen Aga. Maggie estimated a solid fifty years had passed between cleanings. "This place is a wifebreaker, Maggie. You'd need permanent cleaning staff."

"I know."

Boiling water spluttered through the coffee machine, making noise before smoothing out to produce a smooth stream of fragrant liquid. Maggie packed a second shot of coffee into the machine and started that one running too. Milk got warmed in a silver-coloured jug by shooting hot steam through it, and she liked that part of the coffee-making process too. There was café coffee happening in Carmel Walker's spartan kitchen and Maggie took perverse pleasure in knowing Carmel would have called it a frivolous indulgence.

"I'm not saying it couldn't work, this plan of yours," he offered gruffly, after adding half a cup of hot milk and taking a quick gulp. "But there's a lot to think about."

"There's nothing to think about." Not anymore. "I can't do it without the money from the sale of the surrounding land. Not the way I'd want to do it."

"Which is …?"

"All-out high-end luxury. Caterers. Cleaners. Carmel

didn't let the homestead go to ruin because she wanted to, she let it go to ruin because she was one woman and she was already working herself to the bone looking after sheep. The only way this homestead even makes *sense* in this day and age is to open it up and make enough money out of it to pay for the upkeep."

"I'm not disagreeing with you."

She turned to face him, wary as she brought a glossy red cup of coffee to her mouth and sipped, while the silence grew heavy with waiting.

"I've had similar thoughts," he offered finally. "Restore the place and I could fill it with overseas wool buyers on occasion. I have a home already, up in the foothills, and I like it. I wouldn't want to live here. Wasn't exactly thinking weddings, but it makes a certain kind of sense."

Max's approval always had been able to warm her through. "Really?"

"Don't know about the drover's hut to put the honeymooners in." His eyes crinkled. "No electricity. Extremely rustic. The marriage might not last the night."

"Just because it has three walls and only half a roof, doesn't mean it's beyond repair." A new thought occurred to her, shiny bright and beckoning. "What if we formed a partnership? One land title, two owners. You get the land, I get the homestead, and we mostly work around each other and mix business when we need to. Of course, you'd need to buy into the partnership. I'd then use that money to restore the homestead and set up my end."

He didn't say anything for a very long time. He finished his coffee. Maggie finished hers.

"Guess that's a no," she said into the silence. "It was just a thought." Barely formed.

"How much money would you need to do what you want to do with the homestead?" he asked.

"It's hard to say. I'd want to replace the wiring and every last bit of plumbing in the place, and probably add more. Eleven bedrooms might become eight bedrooms if I add ensuites to various rooms. New kitchen and laundry. Paint and wallpaper. And that's before I figure out what has to be restored or replaced. I haven't had a building assessment done on it yet. The foundations may not be as solid as I think."

"Lot of work."

"I'm not afraid of hard work."

"I know. But I'd want your guarantee that you were going to stick around longer than a season and I don't think you can give it. No offence."

He was dead right. As usual. "If it didn't work out you would buy me out and own the lot."

But he didn't seem to like that idea either. "What if I agree to bankroll the homestead restoration for the summer? Same deal as with the land improvements whereby at the end of the three months you make your decision and either stay on or sell the lot to me and go."

"If you bankroll the homestead renovations I may well send you broke too," she muttered. "No, I need to be using my own money, especially on the homestead repair. I don't want to answer to you for the decisions I make, and I don't want to make cost compromises that will undermine what I'm trying to create. It's different to your offer to bankroll the land improvements. The costs there are relatively fixed and quantifiable. Not to mention you'd be the one making those decisions. Should you buy this place in three months' time, you'd be able to justify with perfect clarity the money you've spent."

He eyed her steadily, saying nothing, letting her speak. This too was nothing new for him. He'd always done it. She noticed it more because she now had more to say. "I'm thinking about selling the Melbourne house."

"Thought you didn't want to do that?"

"Yeah, well. Something's got to give. I'd still like to draw up a potential contract of sale with you, actionable at the end of summer with either a firm yes or no from me. You're still my get-out-of-jail-free card if I can't hack it. I'll also investigate splitting the title and see if the rules have changed. If they have, you'll be the first to know, assuming you're interested in land purchase only."

"I am." He eyed her steadily. "But with it I'd want the right to label all agricultural produce coming off the land with the Wirra Station brand. I think you'll find that under ordinary circumstances the brand stays with the woolshed. I may not need the woolshed, but I do want the brand."

"Done." She could live with that. "Although I reserve the right to brand all homestead and function centre–related business with a Wirra Station label too."

"You're good at this."

Maggie smiled. "We should talk price."

"We should." His eyes gleamed. "I'll give you seven thousand a hectare. That's almost double what I'd pay for grazing land not associated with the iconic Wirra Station name."

Maggie's quick mental calculation as to what his offer was worth almost made her choke. She swallowed some coffee and decided that if he could be blasé about the amount of money they were talking about, so could she. "I'm about to get new fencing, tanks troughs and dams," she offered sweetly, never mind that he'd been somewhat instrumental in that negotiation too.

"Which is why I'm offering you a very generous seven thousand per hectare for it." He was enjoying this, she could tell. "Your weed control and fertiliser regime has been non-existent for the past twenty years."

"I know," she conceded. "It's an organic farmer's dream. I'm thinking eight-five per hectare." She closed her eyes and inhaled the scent of fresh coffee. "That's a good deal."

He laughed outright. "The way I see it, not all of your land is prime land. I've already factored the eight hundred hectares of scrub into my absurdly generous offer of seven thousand one hundred dollars per hectare. Also, not everyone's going to be interested in the land without the historic homestead to go with it, or the fact that you intend to use the Wirra Station brand as well."

She opened her eyes and studied him contemplatively through narrowed eyes. "Seven-five will get you collaboration on any Wirra Station promo material I might use."

"Seven-two, and I want priority use of the homestead for two weeks per year, at shearing time, at half the going market rate."

"You're going to house your shearers over here?"

"I'm going to put my buyers over here and give them the ultimate Wirra Station experience. Seven-two, Magpie." He used her old nickname. "That's generous. It's also my final offer on a transaction worth twenty million dollars plus change."

"Done. Do you want to draw up the contract or shall I?" She held out her hand and he took it, his hand hard and calloused in places, but gentle nonetheless. He was smiling again and it reached all the way to his eyes and beyond, but there was something rueful about it, something a little bit self-mocking. "What is it?"

"This is the first time you've reached out to me in over fifteen years," he rumbled quietly. "And it only took the possibility of a twenty-million-dollar deal for you to do it."

Chapter Three

MAX'S FATHER HAD never once questioned Max's business acumen. Until now. They sat at the scarred kitchen table with its sturdy legs and walnut wood grain, and as Max finished outlining his purchase offer for Wirra Station his father's frown became immovable.

His father wasn't one for a waterfall of words when one decent word would do, and at the end of Max's spiel he sat back and ran his hand across his mouth and shaven chin and fixed Max with a bright blue gaze that was so very like his own. "You're offering too much for it."

Max knew that. "I can afford it." He knew how to make the most of his purchase and the branding opportunities that came with it. "It'll work out."

Eventually.

"You're stuck on her," his father offered next, and there was no point asking him who they were talking about and absolutely no point denying it.

"Maybe. Time to find out."

His father nodded as if that was all he needed to know. "She's a prickly little soul."

"With good reason," Max defended. "Carmel never gave

her the time of day."

"Carmel Walker had her own demons to satisfy," his father said quietly. "The Walker women never have been big on mothering. If they were cattle you'd cull 'em."

"I don't want to cull her. Even when she's not around she's still there. She always has been."

"Right." His father stood and headed for the door, reaching first for his boots and then his hat. "Anything else I need to know?"

"Nope. Good talk."

His father snorted. "Good luck."

※

IT TOOK MAGGIE over a week to find the right clean-up crew for the job, and even then they weren't exactly throwing junk out, so much as transferring unwanted items from the homestead to the woolshed and placing them on long trestle tables, ready for auction. The 1914 newspaper declaring Britain and France at war with Germany was not junk. The ancient first aid kit full of rotting bandages and muck-filled tincture bottles was not junk. The tarnished silver service sets—not junk. Some of it would return to the homestead, but not all of it, and right now Maggie's priority was to empty rooms, clean them from top to bottom and then start listing what had to be done.

Ceiling repairs that involved elaborate plasterwork. The stripping of rotting wallpaper that mice had long ago thought tasty—carefully piecing together enough of what was left so as to preserve a large enough sample for reproduction should the heritage foundation insist that the world needed puce-coloured-waratahs-the-size-of-dinner-plates wallpaper.

The electrical wiring—every last bit of it was being replaced along with additional power points and light fittings required in order to comply with current health and safety regulations.

She'd reached out to her old school network for advice and been overwhelmed by the response and the depth of knowledge on offer. Outreach, Jeannie Lamb called it.

Painful, Maggie called it, but she wound back her innate reserve and doggedly put herself and Wirra Station out there.

Jeannie and her husband were now her main building project managers, navigating the many rules and regulatory bodies with expertise. Jeannie's husband in turn had hired a sixty-year-old master carpenter and wood turner who was rapidly proving invaluable.

When Max finally turned up after a two-week absence, there were sixteen people working on the homestead and surrounding buildings. Maggie knew this because she'd finally organised a sign-in book and a column for what everyone would be working on that day. When he found her, head down and arse up in a library lower cupboard, she was wearing pink gloves, a face mask, goggles and a vintage silk headscarf she'd taken from bedroom eight. It wasn't puce. It was jaundice yellow.

"Maggie?"

She backed out of the cupboard and turned to face him, lifting her latex covered hands to her goggles and shifting them on to her forehead as she did so. "Yes?"

He looked. Blinked. Nodded. And seemed to come to some kind of conclusion. "I see you're making progress."

"Money does that." And the banks had been surprisingly eager to let her run up more debt.

"Can I tempt you away from your cupboard cleaning for the afternoon? I want to take a look at some of Wirra Station's old fence lines and throw some ideas at you."

"What kind of ideas?"

"A lot of people when they replace fences nowadays, follow the natural contours of the land rather than divvy land up into rectangles. I could tell you a bit about how that kind of setup might work to your advantage, if you want me to."

"I want you to." She was learning to value expertise and assistance when offered. "Give me five minutes to clean up?"

The look on his face suggested it might take longer but he was gentleman enough to nod and make no mention of it.

"Would you like to read a farm ledger from 1938 while you wait?" She pointed to a club chair and fringed reading lamp. "We think this room must have been the farm office at some point."

"We?"

"Me and Jeannie. Also Sarah from the clean-up crew, Bob the gardener and Elsa the hairdresser think so too."

"Well, who am I to argue?" he murmured and made her

smile.

"Five minutes," she said.

"Leave me with your farm ledger and let me loose on your coffee machine and you can take twenty."

"You're all heart."

"I am, yes."

✶

"I STILL DON'T see how a newlywed couple are supposed to drive up to the drover's hut without breaking their necks," Max mused as he navigated yet another washout in the steep hill track. His four-wheel drive was kitted out for exactly this type of terrain and even it was struggling. He spared a glance for Maggie and smirked at her white-knuckled grasp of the hand grip.

"I see your point," she said.

"Sure, it's pretty enough once you get there. Not as if they'll get any visitors. Privacy is assured, but—"

"Tree down!" she bellowed.

So there was, and it took up a lot of room, but it was still only a wattle tree. Small enough to nudge it off the track using his bull bar and keep going. Where was he? "Can you imagine the health and safety issues associated with putting builders on this site? Not to mention running electricity to it."

"If you're trying to make me reconsider my plans to make this a romantic retreat, good job. *Reaaaally* good job.

Stellar. Although I reserve the right to save any other ideas for phase two of the great Wirra Station restoration plan. Gotta have goals."

He hadn't quite realised how resilient she was in the face of adversity, although maybe he should have. She'd survived this long with minimal encouragement. With backing she could probably conquer the world.

The drover's hut sat on a slope overlooking a protected gully. Further on, jagged rock faces jutted out of the ground and reached towards the sky, their colours ever changing. Weathered orange, ochre and grey, surrounded by the muted green of the Australian bush. He'd spent three days lost in the nearby National Park once, even with all his local knowledge. He'd finally stumbled his way back to the hut in the pitch black of a rainy night and he'd never been more grateful for a leaky roof and three stone walls. The roof had even more holes in it now.

He poked around while Maggie took photos of the hut and the views and some of him as well, unless he was mistaken. "What are the ones of me for?"

"Your mother. I'm not a bad photographer, I'll have you know. I've also started a blog called *Finding Wirra Station*. I post daily and include a lot of pictures about what's happening. It's part of my community outreach plan. Actually, it was Jeannie Lamb's idea, but I'm running with it. The posts that get the most attention are the ones with people in them, doing things, and it doesn't really matter what they're doing. A post about menial cleaning gets just as many comments as the ones showing master craftsmen at work. And don't tell Bob the gardener but he's getting a lot of attention from single ladies of a certain age demographic. There must be something about a man who knows his way around a potting shed. Probably all that nurturing he does."

"So, you want to put a picture of me on your blog and shamelessly exploit me as well? What exactly am I nurturing?"

"You're nurturing my delusions of one day doing something with the hut, although I'm not sure how that's going to translate to a single image. I could always say you're a would-be groom taking some well-earned time out for quiet contemplation before the big event. That'd work."

"You could. And then someone would want to know who the lucky woman was, and I'd say ask Maggie and then the rumours would start to flow. You ready for them? Because you don't look anywhere near ready for them," he told her with a grin.

"Like I said, those photos of you are going straight to your mother and absolutely nowhere else."

"Good choice." He tracked her progress across the rock and continued to watch her as she settled beside him. A lot of people weren't comfortable in Australia's remote bushland, but if Maggie had ever been one of them, she'd since worked her way up to appreciating it. The apprehension she'd shown on the drive up here was gone, replaced by appreciation for the views and the landscape. "Sorry if the drive up here had you scared." He more than anyone knew she had no great love of car travel. "I haven't been up here for a while. The track was worse than I remembered."

She put the camera to her eye and took a couple of shots. "I was the one who suggested it."

Yes, but he was the one with the local knowledge. Supposedly. "Will you have nightmares tonight off the back of it?"

"Hard to say." She lowered the camera and fiddled with it. "I never can tell what will trigger them and I refuse to be a hothouse flower about it. I learned to drive, didn't I?"

"Carmel forced you to learn to drive."

"And she was right to do so. You can't live out here and not drive. Even in the city it helps if you know how to drive."

True enough.

She lifted her face towards his and her chin came up. "I've faced a lot of my fears over time. I even learned to appreciate a good bonfire."

He'd been there for that one—a bush dance for the local Rural Fire Service, complete with bonfire—and if appreciation involved stiff rigidity, frozen features and terrified eyes, then, yeah, she'd learned to appreciate a good bonfire. "Do you ever get someone to take pictures of you doing stuff around the homestead?" Time to change the subject.

"Yes." She nodded. "I have to take ownership of Wirra Station and let people get to know me. Showing my face is an important part of the demystifying process, according to my old school friend, a soon-to-be clinical psychologist. The more approachable I seem and the more open I am with my plans, the more likely people will be to offer their support. At least, that's the plan."

"Come on then." He held out his hand for her camera. "I'll take some shots of you."

She handed him the camera without protest. "Where do you want me?"

"Oh, Maggie, *leading question.* Over there on the rock with the hut behind you."

"Did you just flirt with me?"

"Glad you noticed." From behind the camera, he could look his fill. Point and click, point and click, find the zoom and click and click. Did she have any idea how photogenic she was? "How come you never tried modelling? Surely Carmel had contacts you could have called?"

Her eyes flashed with surprise. Click.

"Carmel was a runway model. I'm five foot two. And a bit. Have you ever seen a five-foot-two-and-a-bit runway model?"

"Still. You have a pretty face. Even when you're scowling."

Which she was doing.

"That's more than enough camera work for you," she muttered.

But he took one more and then another before handing the camera back to her with a grin. "I think you should put one of your scowling photos up for your blog viewers. Call it 'Maggie when Max is around'. It'll help build my mystique."

"Your mystique needs no help from me, Maxxie." She smiled briefly. "I don't think I would have liked being a model. Pretty sure I spent a lot of my school years cringing when people so much as looked at me."

"Maybe you're a late bloomer."

She set the camera aside and leaned back, palms to the warm rock behind her. "I don't want to be a model. I'm quite enjoying what I'm doing now, to be honest. Digging through the history of the station, deciding what furnishings to keep and what can go. So many decisions to make when it comes to which parts of the house I want to keep private and which to make public. I have eleven bedrooms to choose from and I still haven't decided which one to make mine. Not my old one, which is little more than a box room. Not Carmel's, which is nicer, but I'm thinking that one might make a good B and B room. Not the master bedroom—"

"Why not the master bedroom?"

"It's creepy. I go in there to clean it out and last five minutes before fleeing. I take music in with me to cut the silence. I open windows to let the breeze in. Sometimes I last six minutes. There's a big blue basin on a stand beside the door and I've taken to opening the door and dropping all the old newspapers I find in it and then shutting the door again as fast as I can. I do this just in case anyone in there wants to read them. There's no-one in there! Just a big black fireplace, an elaborate gilt mirror, rotting velvet curtains and a canopied wooden bed that will crush you the minute you try to sleep in it. I've seen that movie. I know what happens."

He rubbed his hand over his mouth and jaw and hell if that wasn't a delaying tactic he'd picked up from his father. "Come again?"

"You heard me. And I will push you off this ledge if you make fun of me for this, don't think I won't."

"You won't." It was quite a drop.

"I might."

"Nah, I saw you white knuckling parts of the track on the way up. You still need me to drive you back down."

She screwed up her nose, but there was a smile beneath her scowl. "I do need to take that into consideration."

"Can I see it?"

He'd lost her.

"Will you show me your great-grandfather's room when we get back down?"

She nodded.

"I remember my mother talking years ago about someone around here getting an Elder in to smoke out the spirits. Could be worth a try."

Could be that the room was the repository for all of Maggie's darker feelings about her family too, but he wasn't about to venture his opinion on that. Not when the sun was shining, and Maggie was sitting here confiding in him and making him feel like a goddamn hero just for listening.

For listening.

Later, much later, when they arrived back at the homestead and they'd grazed from the heaped platters of sandwiches Maggie got delivered daily to feed the workers, she led him to the master bedroom and ushered him in.

"Feel it?" she asked.

Er ... hard to say yes without lying. "It's not the warmest room I've ever been in."

"I *know*, right?"

The room was big, the ceilings were high and the heavy curtains did not invite the light in. She started pulling curtains aside and opening windows. She tugged the door to the verandah wide open and jammed a fire poker against it to keep it there. The fireplace was indeed huge. And black, very black, with black marble accents. He loved it. The mirror above it had ripples in it and showed his hair to be a characteristic mess and his shirt to be one of his oldest. He could have stood to make a better impression. He ran his hand through his hair to no effect.

"What are you doing?"

Er ... primping? "It's a room that stays cool in summer though. That never hurts around here."

"Because if you're trying to tame your hair without taking shears to it, give up now. It's never going to happen."

"Aw, Maggie. Don't be like that. It's almost long enough to put up in a top knot."

"And is that something you're likely to do around these parts? You in your top knot and every other grazier hereabouts in short back and sides and a felt hat?"

"I might." He would never. "I'm all about the mystique."

He'd made her laugh, here in this room with her ghosts all around them.

"Look at the bed," she said, and no, nope, he didn't want to look at the bed because the bed would give him ideas and … oh, look.

The bed.

"It's a man's bed," he offered.

"What does that even mean?"

Big. Sturdy. No flowers or unnecessary bits anywhere near it. Except for the velvet canopy which was rust red and grimy with age. "I played in one of these as a kid. Ripped all the sheets off the bed and pegged them up around the sides. I was a jungle explorer and it was my tent."

"You're deliberately trying to make me like this room more," she accused.

"Sometimes it was a boat and I was a pirate of the high seas. Not that I'd ever seen a high sea."

She'd edged a little closer to him. Not something she usually did.

"Tell me about your ancestor who built this place." He knew the basics and not much more, but perhaps in the retelling Maggie would stumble across whatever was bothering her. "Wasn't he the third son of an English earl?"

"Yes. He took to gambling and shady bets like a champion and got deported to Australia for his trouble. Went back to England and brought a wife back with him ten years later. She didn't much care for the place and died giving birth to his only child. A son to carry on the family name. The son's marriage was happier, by all accounts. Wirralong the town was taking shape by then and he married locally. That wife went to Melbourne to have her babies—a boy and a girl and everyone survived. You probably know more about my relatives from that point on than I do."

"My father might. You could have played shipwrecked on an island in here as a kid."

"Or not," she said with a shudder. "You really can't feel the oppression?"

Nope. No oppression to be felt. "What happened to your life back in Melbourne? Your work. Your friends. Significant others?"

"Well, my jobs were always temporary. A teaching day here, a gig as a museum guide there. I have a good friend, Isabella, and I miss her so much. As for my supposed significant other, and you may gape, but I did once have one …"

Max winced at the hurt in her voice. "Not gaping," he said quietly.

"He liked my last name and the doors it opened for him but he turned out to be a fair-weather soul when all was said and done. I don't miss him nearly as much as I should and I guess that speaks for itself."

He was glad. "You want to try something with me? Might give you a different perspective on the people who used to inhabit this room."

"Does it involve boats?"

"No. Close your eyes."

Her eyes widened. "I really try not to do that in this room."

He stepped closer, took her hand in his and pressed her

palm against his heart. "Do you trust me?"

"No reason not to," she mumbled.

"Close your eyes."

She closed her eyes. He was close enough to make out individual eyelashes, softly curled. A sway of her body and he was close enough to feel the puff of her breath against his jaw.

"Are you warmer yet?" he rumbled.

"A little."

This time he was the one to move forward. "How about now?"

"You are definitely warmer than the rest of the room."

He couldn't resist cupping his palm to her cheek and tangling his fingers in the hair at the nape of her neck. Her breath stuttered and he caught it on his lips. "How about now?"

"What are you doing?" she whispered, but she didn't pull away and that was all the encouragement he needed. He'd been told he had a voice that could melt bones. He used it. "I think the master of the house probably didn't mind if his furniture was overpowering and the room held a chill. Either way his wife might cling to him all the more because of it. They made their own heat." He knew where he was going with this, but did she?

And then her hands were in his hair and she was drawing him down, inviting him into a kiss and igniting an inferno with her breathy little groan. He couldn't hold back, he didn't hold back, as he lost himself in her sweetness and the softness beneath his hands.

For so long Maggie had wanted to know what Maxwell O'Connor's kisses would taste like. Sure and strong like the man himself? Playful because he could be that too? He wasn't playing now, though—he was all in and destroying her with single-minded intensity. The rasp of his shirt against her skin, the groan that rumbled out of him, verbal pleasure freely given.

She forced her hands from the silky softness of his hair, dragging them down over his substantial shoulders and the hills and valleys of his chest until she reached the general vicinity of his heart again, that place where he'd encouraged her to touch him.

"Keep going." That voice again, raising goosebumps on her flesh and making her nip his bottom lip lightly in retaliation for his sins against her skin. "Oh, hell yes."

His eyes were closed, his body was rock hard beneath her fingertips, and the urge to slide her hand down over his ribs and across his stomach and keep right on going was almost impossible to resist. It was broad daylight. Anyone could walk past the *two* wide open doors and see what they were doing.

Hard to call what they were doing just a kiss. It was more of a prelude, a promise she'd never encountered before.

She pushed at his chest and he let go and stepped back, eyes blown and an absolutely unrepentant curve to his lips.

"You kiss all the pretty girls like that?" She tried to keep it light and teasing, easy on the shock, and wasn't at all sure she managed it. What did a person say to a kiss that had the power to irrevocably alter one's understanding of the word passion?

"Not all of them, no." He shoved his hands in the pockets of his trousers as if to stop himself reaching for her. Or maybe he did it so that the fabric pulled tight across his really, astonishingly impressive bulge, and she should probably stop looking at it sometime soon or anytime now. Now would be good, because if that was for her, all for her …

Well.

"You know what?" he asked conversationally.

"What?" she croaked, wrenching her gaze north and grasping at what she hoped was a conversational lifeline, only to find him looking around the room with an assessing gaze.

"I like this room a lot," he said. And sauntered out of it.

Chapter Four

"I NEED A haircut," said Max.

"You certainly do." Elsa O'Donoghue ran a practised hand through his mop and studied him in the salon mirror. For kicks, she attempted to twist it into a bun and thankfully failed. It wasn't that bad. Yet. "How short?" she asked.

Max shrugged.

"Okay, let's aim for bedhead. You can pull that off day and night. Do you have time for a wash?"

"Washed it this morning."

"One of these days you're going to let me wash it," she told him. "*And* you're going to enjoy it."

But not today. She sprayed his head with a water squirter, attacked it with a comb and then picked up her scissors. Like him, Elsa was Wirralong born and bred and felt no inclination whatsoever to apologise for it. He knew her family and she knew his. Give him a minute and he could probably remember her middle name, date of birth and the name of the first boy she'd ever kissed. It wasn't him.

"I hear you and Maggie are working miracles out at Wirra Station," Elsa said and started cutting. "Stay still."

A snort and a flash of pink alerted him to the presence of someone else in the salon. He turned his head a fraction and got Elsa grabbing both sides of his skull and setting him straight again.

"I have toddlers in this chair who can stay stiller than you."

"Did you give him the booster seat?"

The voice clued him in. "Hey, Maggie. Elsa was just trying to gossip about you. I gave her nothing."

"Sweetie pie, I already know all about the kiss," said Elsa smugly. "I made her run through the lead-up three times. In vivid detail."

"Maggie, did you kiss and tell?" he rumbled, unapologetically delighted.

"O'Connor, if you don't keep your head straight so I can cut properly, I'm going to get the clippers out and run stripes through your hair for the hell of it," chided Elsa.

"What else did she say about my kisses?" Max asked, sitting very, very still. "Have they ruined her for all other men? Because that was the underlying intention."

"She's *right there*. Ask her yourself."

"I'm not answering that," said Maggie and came into view in the mirror. She wore sand-coloured trousers and a pink tank top with a picture of a cartoon grasshopper on it. Her hair was tied back in a messy bun and her oversized sunglasses perched on her head. She wore no make-up, as far as he could tell, and she still managed to look more appealing than any woman he'd ever met. "Elsa, I need your signature on a release form for the photos we took the other day. These are the ones I want to use."

Elsa stopped snipping as Maggie held up two pics. All Max saw was the back of them, and he was determined not to be curious, but then Maggie showed them to him next. "You can look too seeing as I'm interrupting your hair cut," she said.

"Pretty." Elsa was a beauty and Maggie had been the client in the chair and whether they'd been posing for the pic or not, the warmth between the women showed through. "Where's it going?"

"On the Wirralong Homestead website under 'Services'."

"That's me. At your service," said Elsa cheerfully.

"You could be at *my* service a little more solidly," offered Max, and wore their looks of disbelief and amusement with equanimity. Elsa might have been holding a really sharp pair of scissors but she wasn't a mean one … was she?

"Don't you know to be *nice* to your hairdresser?" Maggie said.

Was that a thing? God help him. He eyed Elsa balefully. "You already know more than I do about what's going on at Wirra Station. Why did you even ask me?"

"Always nice to get both sides of the story," his soon-to-be-ex hairdresser said cheerfully. "We've been trying to get to the bottom of the reason for your kiss all week. Was it spontaneous? Did the ghost make you do it? Are you courting?"

He didn't whimper, but it was close. "Aren't you meant

to be cutting hair?"

"Yes. Aren't you meant to be cutting hair?" Maggie echoed and Elsa smirked.

"An echo. That's so cute. Where do you want me to sign?"

"Right here." They used the bench in front of him for a desk, a woman on either side of him, and, seriously, who did business like this?

He thought it.

He wasn't quite stupid enough to say it.

"Have dinner with me," he said instead.

Not the best move when surrounded by two women and wearing a black plastic cape that choked around his neck. Not exactly a position of raw power and persuasion, was it?

"O'Connor, I thought you were smoother than this," Elsa said.

He was. "Sorry, Red. I was talking to Maggie. Which … usually ends badly, frankly."

"And yet you still want to take her to dinner?"

"Business to discuss."

"Uh huh." Elsa the sceptical signed her image away and stepped back behind him.

Maggie collected the papers and stashed them in her bag but she didn't move away and instead pinned her doe-brown eyes on him. "I'm trying to have dinner at every restaurant in town, so I know which ones to recommend. Or, if I end up listing them all on the website, how best to describe them. So far I've tried the Brasserie, the Chinese restaurant, and the

Travellers Rest Café. I want to try the Fork and Spoon on Thursday night. I hear good things and I'm not opposed to company. Are you free then?"

He could be. He nodded. Elsa cursed and Maggie laughed.

"Max, if you don't keep your head still—"

"Will you still go out with me if I end up with a buzz cut, Margaret Mary?"

She tilted her head to one side and studied him thoughtfully. "You do have a beautifully shaped head."

"That's a thing women look for?" Because ... seriously?

"It is if she's your hairdresser and she's considering giving you a crew cut," Elsa told him. "It'd make people focus on your eyes and features." She used her hands to pull the hair back from his forehead and studied him in the mirror again. "How is he from the side?"

Maggie stepped away from the counter and he resisted the urge to turn his head. "Unrelentingly perfect."

Maggie sounded glum and for some reason Max cheered right up. He wasn't anywhere near perfect, they both knew that, but he could stand to hear some praise from this woman from time to time—even if it was about his looks. It was a start.

Maggie left and Elsa settled to her job with a focus and a lack of questions he was grateful for. Only when the plastic cape had been removed and she was checking him over for length, scissors in hand, did she speak again. "You realise it's brutally obvious to anyone who knows you and sees you with

Maggie that you're completely into her?"

Yeah, well. He didn't much care. "It's not obvious to her."

✹

MAGGIE WOKE WITH a gasp or a scream. Hard to tell in the darkness, hard to know what was real, but the wild thrashing of her heart was real, and the sweat that slicked her skin was real, and the trembling of her hands was real as she brought them to her face and slowly eased her palms up and over her hair.

The psychologist said touch would ground her, even her own touch would do. Feel her face, her head, down to the back of her neck to massage the tightly clenched muscles there. Breathe in, breathe deep. Open her eyes and turn on a light and let the lingering aftermath of the nightmare leave her.

Maggie had her post-nightmare routine down pat.

A shower first, to scrub imaginary soot and dirt from her skin. Not too hot and not for too long, and no attempting to rub her skin raw. A new nightgown, soft and sensual and altogether grown up. Not for her the boy shorts and T-shirt tops, although she often wished she could wear them. But she needed the reminder that many years had passed and clothes more associated with her childhood didn't help with that. A nightgown if it was before four am and she thought she had a snowball's chance of getting back to sleep. Day clothes after four because she may as well accept that her day had started with a bang and get up to greet it.

She'd claimed a corner room for her own. It had north-facing French doors, two tall, sashed windows facing west, and a bathroom next door. The kitchen and the coffee maker were a million miles away at the other end of the house, but it was a small price to pay for privacy, a cross-breeze, a pressed-metal ceiling and, arguably, the finest small fireplace in the homestead. Carmel had used it as a formal sitting room and Maggie had always liked it.

As a bedroom, with freshly painted pale olive-green walls and off-white ceiling, softly burnished floorboards, and a red-and-green Murano hanging light, it was superb. A custom-made sideboard held an old-fashioned record player and a record collection that spanned half a century or more.

Music was not grounding. Music could make a person soar, but it could also place a person in time and convey mood. Steer a mind away from memories clamouring to surface.

'Breakfast at Sweethearts'. A café for the downhearted and displaced and a song about being grateful for small mercies. She set it to playing and opened the French doors to let the last of the night air in. Bob the gardener had already promised her some night-scented honeysuckle and sweet rocket for this end of the garden. Bob was enthusiastic about her plan to hold weddings here and open the homestead up to bed and breakfast visitors.

One of her dearest friends had promised to visit soon,

full of enthusiasm for Maggie's new business plans. Support for the project was growing.

And then there was Max, who made no secret about wanting Wirra Station and she was having no luck whatsoever when it came to splitting the title—in spite of her thirty-six page proposal outlining the benefits. Her lawyer contacts were on it and if *they* couldn't make it happen, no-one could.

Which left her spending money as if she had an unlimited supply of it and Max racking up herbicide and seed purchases on her Henderson's account, and putting man hours and tractor fuel and equipment hire into pasture renewal, because she sure as sunrise had neither the equipment nor the skilled manpower to do it herself. Max was working under the assumption that the land would soon be his—it was the only reason she could think of for his unstinting support and generosity.

And she wasn't at all sure it was going to happen.

Max had always featured in her nightmares. Eyes blown wide, dancing flames against the black. Stark fear and more strength than he should have had as he'd wrenched the car door open and dragged her out. Only, nowadays, in her daydreams, they were older and she wasn't trying to get away from him at all. Instead, she was kissing him and kissing him and writhing against him and *owning* him.

The heat of his skin beneath her greedy hands. Warm of heart and so utterly open, and he was like that in real life too. She'd been trying to ignore his romantic interest in her but it was hard to do when he was so straightforward about it.

It was past time to remind him that she came with complications.

The scarring on her lower abdomen hadn't tipped Richard off to the fact that she probably couldn't have children and he hadn't taken it at all well when she'd told him. She doubted Max would be any different.

Then again, Richard hadn't been begging her to *hold still for fuck's sake because if you don't your stomach's going to fall out.*

Maybe Max already knew what those old injuries meant. Maybe she could mention it tonight at dinner, slip it into the conversation, all casual-like.

Lovely.

Laughter escaped, a helpless bubble of bleak humour. She didn't know what time it was, but she needed coffee and breakfast, and she needed it now. Then maybe she'd slip outside to greet the dawn and think about happier times, like the laughter yesterday as her cleaning crew unearthed a hidden cellar full of wine-turned-to-vinegar. To Maggie's knowledge, not a drop of liquor had ever passed Carmel's lips. The door to the cellar had been hidden behind a heavy rosewood cupboard that had taken four men to shift.

She had the video of the opening of the first bottle and the hardy souls willing to taste it. The looks on their faces and the fresh laughter as they spat it straight back out. Bottle after bottle until finally they found a good one. They'd looked up the brand name, but they couldn't find any mention of it online.

They'd drawn straws to decide who was going to be the canary in the coal mine and drink a full glass of it.

Bob the gardener had been their canary and Maggie was pretty sure he'd had several willing helpers when it came to finishing the bottle, but no-one had died, so they'd opened another one and somewhere along the way she'd had a party on her hands.

This morning she would ban all comers from the wine cellar and get her work crew to slide the rosewood cupboard back in place until she figured out what to do with her vintage bottles of vinegar and wine.

Would customers pay good money to come down here and choose a bottle, and then choose again until they got a good one? Was that a thing? Like gold digging or sapphire hunting? The lure of striking it rich?

That could definitely be a thing, and she mentally added wine-tasting weekends to her line-up of Wirra Station offerings.

✸

THE DAY PASSED slowly and Maggie spent far too much time wondering what to wear and far too little time on the renovation matters at hand. She spent almost two hours getting ready for a dinner date in the sleepy town of Wirralong, population 5790 and counting. She was overdressed, underprepared and had applied way too much make-up to her face in the hope of making herself look older and more sophisticated, and why? Because that was the image she wanted to portray? Because she thought Max, who was in business partnership with an Italian model, would like it? An Italian model Maggie had never seen but nonetheless decided looked like Sophia Loren.

What did that say about her other than *Maggie, you're trying too hard and you're way too insecure*?

Story of her life.

She'd mopped almost all of her make-up back off when she heard the sound of a vehicle approaching.

It wasn't Max's farm truck. It was a low-slung sedan with gleaming chrome and ruby-red paint and if that was Max's ride she didn't have *nearly* enough make-up on. With a growl of frustration she swapped out her shoes—those sensible ones she'd decided would do—for sky-high bits of glossy stiletto temptation. They went some way towards matching the car.

Who cared if she could barely walk in them?

She watched as Max emerged from the car and made his way to the door. He was wearing a suit and she'd bet every last cent that it was Italian and made by some superstar designer, probably using wool grown here. His shirt collar was stiff and white and he wasn't wearing a tie, and she undoubtedly needed a new lipstick colour for the evening—something altogether sophisticated.

Coral nude, coral satin, coral pearl, and hallelujah! Semi-sheer and sticky glossy ruby red.

Her dress was high in the waist and made the most of her

barely there curves and shapely legs. She'd pinned her hair up in its trademark messy bun that took no time at all to deliver but usually looked good. Fancy shoes and lipstick was the best she could do without rethinking her entire outfit, and, frankly, she didn't have time to.

She met him at the door, opening it wide, unaccountably nervous, and was gratified when he seemed at a loss for words. His eyes, on the other hand, suggested a liking for what he saw.

"Hi," she murmured. Brilliant start.

"Hi."

They were *on fire* on the conversational front.

"You ready?" he asked, and she was as ready as she ever would be with Max O'Connor standing there looking like he'd stepped from the pages of a glossy magazine, every last inch of him immaculate, from his freshly cut hair to the tips of his shoes. He was the boy who'd pulled her from the car wreck when they were kids. The teen who'd dumped her in the water trough when she'd worked too long in the heat. He was the man of her dreams last night and it hadn't all been nightmares. Was she ready for him? Finally?

"I'm ready," she said and pulled the door shut behind her.

High heels and gravel weren't her favourite combination and she vowed to find an easier surface for brides to navigate when moving from homestead to vehicle. Another small detail for her to-do list that would invariably involve a whole lot of money she didn't quite have.

She reached the edge of the verandah, slipped off her shoes and headed barefoot down the steps.

He swept her into his arms before her toes hit the gravel, and she huffed a strangled laugh.

"Your solutions are always physical ones," she said as she opened the car door and he dumped her inside. "Why is that?"

His face was mere inches from her own, his scent clean and heady, his skin smooth from a recent shave. "Preference." His gaze skittered to her lips and then away and then he withdrew and shut the door on her.

The car was full of leather and luxury and there was no denying she was used to it from the life she'd left back in Melbourne. She just hadn't expected it from this man who drove around most days in a beat-up old truck and wore steel-caps and faded denims and ragged tees like a second skin.

"You didn't have to go to all this trouble to impress me. It's just dinner," she said as he drove towards town.

His expression hardened, just a fraction, and he spared her a glance before turning his attention back to the track. "You didn't have to dress up either. But you did."

"If I'm going to run a luxury events venue, I'm going to need to project a certain image. I'm practising. What's your excuse?"

"Hell if I know, Maggie. Do men usually dress down when taking you out to dinner? Is that how they respect you? Or is it that you're so busy clinging to the image of me you already have in your head that there's no room for anything else?"

She could feel her heart thudding uncomfortably in her chest. He always had been able to see to the bottom of her and back, no matter what uncomfortable truths she tried to hide from him. Only these days he called her on them. Honest and blunt and not afraid to examine his reality.

"You look beautiful," she offered, trying to find her truth for him. "Comfortable, confident, amazing. Whatever people call it when they look at someone and get flustered and short of breath and awkward for that person's attention. And then when they have that attention they get even more awkward and say all the wrong things when what they should have said was you're always memorable, no matter what you wear, but that suit looks particularly good on you tonight and I'm glad you could join me for dinner. Even if I cock it up. Which ... you should probably assume I will."

If she hadn't already.

She couldn't look at him. She stared at her hands instead, the tightly clasped mess of them and the newfound callouses that came of hard household cleaning and not enough aftercare.

"I wore a suit because I don't want you looking at me and thinking of the boy who made all the mistakes with you when we were growing up." His words came out of nowhere and hit with the force of a freight train. "If I could erase every bad memory of me you have, I'd do it; but I can't, so instead I'll plaster other memories over the top of them until we're good. That's why I'm doing this. It's all I *can* do."

"That's ... Max, you don't have to do that. You're already far more than I deserve and the first thing I need to get off my chest tonight is that I'm not making much headway with splitting the land deed. I have good lawyers on it and they're getting nowhere. Meanwhile I'm spending money like I have a license to print it, I'm probably going to have to sell the Melbourne house within a month in order to pay my bills, and I don't know where that leaves you and me, because what if I decide to stay? What happens then?"

"I don't mind if you stay."

"You might not get the land if I do."

"Then we'll figure out another way of getting on with business." He sent her a fleeting smile as the car crunched its way over a cattle grid and the gravel beneath the tyres made way for treacherous red dirt. "I like the thought of you sticking around, whether it interferes with my expansion plans or not. You want to own this place, then own it."

It wasn't only his physicality that was blunt.

A row of downed fence posts caught her attention, and she didn't want to argue with him, she really didn't, but if she ever *was* going to own this place heart and soul, she needed to speak up.

"The fencers started work on the last of the inner paddocks today. They said you told them I wanted two hundred acres around the homestead fenced off."

"You do."

"You also gave them new fence lines to follow."

"The old ones made no sense. May as well do it right. We talked about it, remember?"

Again, she agreed in principle. But his utter lack of consultation had her grinding her teeth. "When you wanted to start weed spraying, you rang and explained the why and where of it. You favoured direct drilling of pastures and explained why, and I appreciated the time you took to lay it out for me. You were teaching me, just like you said you would, even though I said I wasn't that interested. You insisted. Yes, we shifted some of the internal fence lines, but not these ones. And then today, for a decision you *knew* I'd be interested in weighing in on, you carved up my land as if yours was the only decision that mattered."

"It wasn't like that."

"Then what was it like?"

"It was about animals having access to windbreaks and creek water, and I cut off thirty acres at most and added it right back by carving out more acreage for you beyond the woolshed, so that you got the willows and the stand of ironbark because I figured your brides and your photographers could use those backgrounds if they wanted to. Was I wrong?"

He wasn't wrong and she didn't know how to explain her objection. She could see the division he had in mind and there was sense in it. Henderson's men took orders from him, the fencing teams were run by him, and she'd not objected to it. And yet. "This is borderland, Max. Your business needs smacking up against mine. Why didn't you *ask* me about it?"

He had the grace to look discomfited. "We can drive the new fence lines now if you want."

"I've already done it with Bob. Who agrees with you, by the way. And I like the new division, don't get me wrong. I'd have liked it a whole lot better had I made that decision with you, and now I'm going to have to put in a whole new application for subdivision with the heritage foundation and that's not something I particularly want to do."

"Noted."

Noted, but not sorry.

"I overstepped," he said. "It won't happen again. And leave the subdivision application as is for now."

"You realise I'm huffing at you on the inside," she said.

"I hadn't, no, but I appreciate the warning. Let me make it up to you."

"And how might you do that?"

"There's a farming family south of us, the McMillans. Do you know them?"

"No."

"They have three daughters, twins who must be eighteen or so now and another a year or so older. They're hard workers—those girls have worked the floor of my shearing shed for years, come shearing time. I'd like you to meet them. See if they're interested in taking on your housekeeping role between them."

"You want me to give people you know a job. That's your apology for running roughshod over my boundaries?"

"My apology and my gift. You haven't seen them work."

"You have a silver tongue. When did that happen?"

"Somewhere between the end of school and acquiring my suit." He smiled and it was contagious.

"Is that suit made from O'Connor wool?"

"Of course."

"Might there one day be Wirra Homestead scarves made out of Wirra Station wool?"

"That could be arranged."

"You're forgiven your appalling lack of fence consultation."

"You should have held out for throw rugs too."

She should have. They were nearing the fork in the road and the track that led to the other entrance to Wirra Station. The entrance Maggie never used and Max had better sense than to take, what with her in the car.

"What were you even doing there, that night?" she asked as they drove past the turnoff.

He knew what she meant. And if he didn't she'd spell it out for him, but she didn't think she'd have to.

"That night?" He slid her a searching glance and then turned his attention back to the road. "I was taking the shortcut home. I had to be home by dark. That was the rule and I'd run out of daylight."

Such a simple reason. "Bet you wish you'd headed home earlier."

"I've never wished that," he offered quietly and shut her up completely.

She fidgeted with the inexpensive bracelet on her wrist. "What had you been doing to lose track of time?" she asked because she was a glutton for punishment and because she genuinely wanted to know what he'd been doing just before her world had gone up in flames.

"I was at Chambers Creek with Rosie Daniels and her brother."

She didn't know either of those names. "Doing what?"

"Smoking. Only did it that once. Copped enough smoke inhalation on the way home to put me off it for life. For a while there I wondered if you losing your parents was my punishment for lying to mine, but I couldn't make it fit."

"That's because it makes no sense."

"My father agreed. Right after he grounded me and took away my quad bike privileges for a month. Do you know how long it takes to walk from my parents' place to the farm gate to catch the school bus? An hour, fifteen minutes. But I wasn't sleeping much back then and the walk, or the run, gave me exercise and helped clear my head ready for school, so maybe he was on to something."

His memories gave her pause and made her chest ache. His truth was different to hers, but also similar in some ways. "Your father and Carmel must have been reading from the same play book. I've never worked so hard as I did the first few days I came to live here. But I slept better for it."

She took a breath and spelled out her truth surrounding those minutes before the accident. "We were coming in from Melbourne. My mother hadn't wanted us to visit, but my father insisted. Carmel was the only family he had left and he was fond of her in a way that my mother wasn't. My parents were arguing when we crashed. Pretty sure that was the cause of it. Speed, hot tempers, a tight bend and a dirt road."

She'd never told anyone that before. Not the investigators who'd questioned her, not the man she'd almost married, and certainly not Carmel. "Nothing to do with your newfound smoking habit at all. Anyway." She looked at his hands on the steering wheel and then to the road up ahead. Looking forward, not back. "There is one more thing I want to say that touches on that night and our ongoing negotiations about who gets what part of Wirra Station going forward, and then I'll stop."

"I'm listening."

"I can't have children. That night took care of that. So, in the Last Will and Testament I signed earlier this week, I left everything to you."

Chapter Five

BY THE TIME they got to the Fork and Spoon and had drinks and starters in front of them Max still didn't trust himself enough to speak more than a couple of words at a time. Because if he did, his temper would have spilled out all over the place, starting with 'screw this world and every last bit of unfairness in it', and finishing somewhere around 'what the hell are you contemplating your own death for?'

Instead, he let Maggie fill the silence with increasingly halting conversation about her thoughts on flying wedding caterers and food in, as opposed to sourcing food and catering talent from Wirralong and nearby towns. The service at the Fork and Spoon eatery was impeccable—far beyond that of a regular sleepy country town—and it wasn't the food's fault that it tasted like ash.

He just wasn't in the mood for it.

He nodded in the right places and said the right things, but his mind was barely keeping up with the plans for the chef to head out to Maggie's homestead the following week to advise her on her fledgling kitchen setup. She offered to pay the guy for his time and expertise and he shook his head and laughed and said his advice came free, a gesture that earned him brownie points with Max, but only because he knew the man was happily married.

A kindness for a kindness, and Max looked on in silence as Maggie offered up a tour of her newfound wine and vinegar cellar to the chef. It was just good business and Max sat back and let her tend to it and tried to get her earlier words out of his head.

Leaving Wirra Station to him in her will was a grand gesture to be sure, but it made him itch.

He wanted nothing more than for her to look forward, rather than back, when she looked at him, but in true Maggie fashion she'd overdone it. Looking forward towards a lonely death and making him a *benefactor,* no less.

He couldn't stand the thought.

"You're very quiet," she said, after the main meals had come and gone and he'd pushed food into his mouth and couldn't have said what it was. "You're making me work hard on the conversation front and let's face it, that's never been my forte. A little help here."

"You could adopt." Bitten off words to suit his mood. He watched her blink and caution creep into her sweetly pretty face.

"I really don't think this is the place—"

"You started it. You could foster children or marry someone who already has children or marry and have no children at all and still be part of a family unit, but for some reason none of those options seem to have crossed your mind." He wasn't a fiery soul, in the grand scheme of things, but Maggie always had driven him to extremes. "You're looking forward, good for you, but *why the hell have you mapped out your life all the way up to and including your death*? Who does that? How about you back up a few decades, Maggie, and let life happen?"

"I made a will, not a death wish. And I really don't see your problem."

She was his problem, and always had been. "Wills traditionally provide for family."

"*Thank you, Einstein.* But if you care to look around, you will see that *I don't have any* and you saved my life once."

"Then thank me like you mean it and be done with it! Don't you pay me for that, Maggie. Don't you ever." He had a temper when crossed, fierce and biting, but this wasn't about him being crossed, it was about Maggie settling for less and accepting it as her due. And that was just not on. "Why can't you have children?"

"I don't want to talk about this here. I don't want to talk about this ever."

"Funny. I could have sworn you brought the subject *up*."

"So you'd know where I stand with succession planning, if I can't sell the land to you outright. You once said you wouldn't lease from me for anything less than twenty years because of the work you'd have to put into the land. Well the work is getting done and being paid for—presumably by you, because I've yet to see a bill—and that bothers me because I have very little idea how (a) I'm going to pay for it and (b) how I'm going to stock the place and run it the way it should be run once you've finished doing whatever you're doing to it. I want you on board, to buy or to lease, and I mistakenly thought that if you knew the whole lot would be yours one day that we might come to some kind of arrangement in the meantime." She had a stubborn set to her mouth that he remembered of old.

"We can sort something out. That bit's true," he grated. "But you sure as hell won't have to forfeit your future for it. Why can't you have children of your own?" He'd ask it again and again until she gave him the details.

"Because I don't have a uterus, you absolute moron."

"Do you have ovaries?"

"One."

"Does it work?"

"I am not talking with you about this."

"You've finished all the business you wanted to do here, haven't you?" Damn right she had. He'd watched her do it. "You want coffee?"

"No."

"Dessert?"

"No."

Good neither did he. He motioned for the bill and reached for his wallet, but she stayed him with her hand on his arm.

"I'm paying."

Hell would freeze over first. He threw enough notes on the table to cover the meal and leave a healthy tip and then stood up. The car was just outside the door and he scowled at it, her earlier comments about her parents arguing in the car coming back to haunt him. She had high heels on but it wasn't as if the main drag was all that long. The road forked and they were standing in the middle of that fork. They could walk one of the tines and cut across and walk the other. "Let's walk."

She looked at the car and sighed, but fell into step beside him and he adjusted his stride accordingly. The breeze was up but it was a hot one, blowing in across the plains and bringing the dry dust of baked earth with it. He was used to it—this was his home—but there was a bead of sweat on Maggie's forehead and those shoes of hers weren't meant for walking. When they got to the church he stopped and leaned against the wall, hands in his pockets to stop him from reaching for her. They were eye to eye now, with the low stone fence at his back and the church behind that, and maybe he could siphon some peace from it. "Talk to me," he said. "Tell me why you're not even considering embryo harvesting and IVF and surrogacy, or adoption or fostering or even just finding someone to share your life with."

She looked past him, towards the church, lips tightening.

"Is this about the guy you left behind in Melbourne? He throw you over because you couldn't have children, is that it?"

A tiny nod.

"Screw him."

"You wouldn't want to marry a woman who couldn't have children either."

"You don't know that." He didn't even know that and he'd been chewing on it all night. "Yes, I want to be a father one day, but it's not as if I'll be the one giving birth. If the person I want to spend my life with couldn't have children there are other options on the table." He'd already mentioned some of them. "If that person didn't *want* children, well, that would be a different discussion." One that made words stick in his throat, never mind the need to voice them. "Maggie, do you want to be a mother or not?"

"I don't know." He could barely hear her. "I don't think I'd be very good at it."

"You'd learn."

Another jerky nod and he didn't know quite where that left him. Heart jerking around on a string was as good a description as any.

"All I'm saying is that you might want to keep your options open so that one day when you wake up and there's someone beside you, you haven't already made promises to me that you no longer want to keep. I don't want to hurt you. I never have. I'm trying to protect you."

"From myself?" Finally she met his gaze and hers was steady and searching.

If the shoe fit… "Try putting yourself first, for once. That might help."

"Maybe I *was* trying to protect myself by telling you I couldn't have children. Maybe I have more self-preservation in me than you think."

He raised an eyebrow in invitation.

She raised her chin. "You kissed me. You offered to marry me. It's clear you're interested in me and not just because of business. When Richard found out I couldn't carry children he accused me of misleading him. I've no intention of misleading you too, so I told you what you needed to know and now you can back off, no harm done."

"Oh, I get it. You expect me to be an arsehole like him. No more kisses for your bad barren self, is that it? No need then for either of us to dwell on how good it felt."

"*Yes*. That's exactly what I think is going to happen now, so will you please just get on with it?"

There was more than one way to be a bastard.

He pushed off the wall and leaned forward, his mouth finding hers with unerring accuracy, and it was soft and startled and too sweet for words. He kept his hands to himself so that she could push him away easily enough if she wanted to, but she didn't.

Nor did she reach for him.

He pulled back reluctantly, a nibble here, a ragged sigh there. "Find another reason to push me away if you need one, barren girl. Because I'm still right here."

✹

THE EVENING WASN'T meant to end like this, Maggie thought, as he drove her home in silence. Max wasn't supposed to brood quite so spectacularly, for starters. Throughout dinner and afterwards, as if he were struggling to come to some momentous conclusion involving his future and hers. He wasn't supposed to have kissed her and set her world alight all over again and the tension in the car wasn't supposed to be so thick as to limit breathing.

He was supposed to be leaving her alone, not accusing her of pushing him away. He wasn't supposed to be still within reach.

He'd come to her rescue so many times already and she couldn't bear the thought of him trying to rescue her again because he thought she might be in need of it.

Like the time she'd been the strange girl on the local school bus—last day before summer holidays and completely out of place with her straw hat and wool blazer and tartan skirt that fell almost to her ankles. It had been boarding school policy that all students had to wear full school uniform to and from their place of residence and Maggie had sagged beneath the weight of it. Last to get on the bus and second last to get off it. Maybe Carmel had squared it with the driver or maybe she hadn't, but no-one ever asked who she was and the driver always stopped at Wirra Station to let her off. Max would always be the only other kid left by then and she remembered this one particular time … the time she'd vowed to be friendly and ended up even more tongue-tied than ever … it had been thirty-eight degrees in the shade and he'd been the one to speak first.

"Doesn't anyone ever come to pick you up?" he'd asked as he'd glanced from her shiny black shoes to her beribboned hat, and then to the gate and the long red-dirt drive that would take her to the house.

"Got to remember what day it is for that," she'd said with what she'd hoped was languid nonchalance.

"Get off at my stop and I'll give you a lift up to your house," he'd offered, but she'd refused him and said something along the lines of there being no need for that and that she liked walking—because she was an idiot, and because she'd been trying to prove she was tough enough to belong to Wirra Station.

She'd stepped off that damn bus and hauled a bag over each shoulder and made it over the cattle grid without falling on her face.

He'd picked her up two kilometres in from the front gate and she'd slung her bags in the back of his beat-up old truck and got into the passenger seat without a word, limp with sweat and tight-lipped with the effort that came of not breaking down and crying in front of him.

There's been no-one at the house to greet her and she'd waved it off as normal. It *was* normal. The house was never locked, she'd said. The new black-and-tan pup waiting nervously on the verandah looked friendly enough.

He'd cut the engine, got out and called the dog and reduced it to a puddle of ecstasy at his feet, courtesy of his attention, and then picked up her bags and walked her to the front steps of the old sandstone homestead.

"Call if you need anything," he'd said with a smile she'd found altogether overwhelming, and then he'd left. It had taken twenty minutes for the dust to settle. Half an hour for her heartbeat to return to normal.

She didn't think saying goodbye to him tonight was going to feel much different.

"You said you had a house in the foothills." Maggie was proud of the way her voice came out even.

He studied her through hooded eyes. "I do."

"I'd like to see it."

"Now?"

"Yes."

"Why?"

He wasn't making this easy for her. "New memories to replace the old, you said. And you dropping me off and driving away is a memory I already have."

He said nothing in reply, but the turnoff to Wirra Station came and went and when finally they pulled up in front of the dark shape of a house, it was a silhouette she'd never seen before. The outline was low-slung and modern and a light came on as they reached a wide side door. There was foyer space for boots and coats and she stepped out of her shoes so as not to sound loud on the shiny wooden floor. The living, dining and kitchen areas had been combined into one big space with plenty of windows to the northeast and to the west. Leather chesterfields and club chairs dominated one part of the room, a wooden dining table and eight chairs waited to be filled. Not the home of a man who didn't value company, or family, or space to spread, and yet somehow he'd kept the proportions inviting and the overall impression one of casual, functional warmth.

"This wasn't here six years ago," she said, more of an invitation for him to talk than an observation of any significant merit.

"No. I had it built when I came back from overseas. I had the money and I wanted my independence."

He didn't seem inclined to expand on that. Maggie's gaze fell on several decanters with varying amounts of amber liquid sitting on a sideboard. "I could use a nightcap." She could use a plan when it came to what she was doing here in the first place, but she didn't have one.

He poured her a drink and reached into a fridge below the sideboard for a bottle of fizzy water for himself.

"You're not drinking?"

"Not if I'm driving you back to your place tonight, no."

Ah. "How many bedrooms do you have?"

"One."

"Seems a little short-sighted given the size of your living room."

"Okay, I have four, but only one's set up as a bedroom. I like my privacy and it gets me out of offering visiting buyers a room when they come to see the operation. It's part of the reason for my interest in what you're looking to do with Wirra Station. It'd suit me to have people stay there on occasion. It'd be good for business."

One bedroom. She sipped at the drink he put in her hand with a little more enthusiasm than was necessary. They didn't communicate well with words, and never had, and it didn't seem as if a couple of scorching kisses were ever going to change that. A more confident woman might walk over there and relieve him of his water, pour him a different drink and let him make of that what he would. A less confident woman wouldn't have invited herself to his home in the first place. But he'd kissed her once and then she'd told him the last of her secrets, and then he'd kissed her again and told her he was going nowhere and what did that *mean* exactly? She took a deep breath and looked for a chair and decided a corner spot on the chesterfield looked comfortable. It was too long for her legs so she tucked them up beneath her, a pillow at her back and the arm wide enough to set her drink on. The leather was butter soft. She'd have killed for some soothing music but words would have to do. "You kissed me. Twice."

"Not a crime."

"You've been nothing but supportive, helpful and enthusiastic about my plans for Wirra Station."

"It pays to get on with my neighbours, although not all of them are insane enough to write me into their *will*."

"You're really hung up on that, huh."

"It's self-limiting." He turned his back on her and reached for a decanter and poured with a heavy hand. She didn't know whether to be encouraged or concerned that she'd driven him to drink. He'd asked her to marry him, even if he had couched it in businesslike terms.

"I'm beginning to think you like me," she said finally, and he finished off his drink in one biting swallow before turning to glare at her.

"How is this *possibly* news?"

"We have a ... bond ... a shared intimacy if you like, that neither of us wanted, but it's there just the same. Doesn't mean you look at me and like what you see. I thought you looked at me and saw weakness." She *was* weak. But she was working on it. "And while that would be understandable and explain your overdeveloped desire to help me, it doesn't explain the kisses."

"I will never again underestimate your ability to overlook the obvious," he muttered. "By all means, try and explain away the kisses without addressing the fact that *I like you*."

"Well, you may have a latent subconscious desire to wallpaper over our earlier shared experience with something more positive and life affirming, like kisses. Or sex."

He closed his eyes and rubbed at the frown between his eyebrows. "I see."

"Or maybe you're just bored and not particularly choosy and I'm convenient."

"I'm not bored, I'm extremely choosy, and liking a woman who's as mad as a meat axe is in no way convenient."

"No need to get insulting."

He opened one eye, possibly to check if she was still there, and when she was he eyed her balefully.

"Or maybe—"

And then he was kissing her again and there was no room for talking, and one hand was in her hair, tilting her head just so—and, oh, he knew exactly what to do when given free rein—and his other hand was on the couch beside her and his shoulders were warm and corded beneath her hands and either he was extremely committed to his self-appointed task of shutting her up or he simply liked kissing her.

And touching her.

Silently encouraging her to offer her body up for the taking, what with the kissing and the touching, and what did it matter that they couldn't speak to one another without being at cross purposes? Verbal communication was overrated.

"I like you. The question is, do you like me?" he murmured, and there he went again. Talking. "Because I'd like to establish this beyond reasonable doubt before continuing."

She was kissing him, wasn't she? Spending time with him, inviting herself into his home. Bequeathing sheep stations to him upon her demise. Wasn't it obvious? "I like you."

"Are you under the influence of alcohol?"

"You saw what I drank tonight. I'm under the influence of *you*." And if he would just stop talking there could be nakedness involved and skin on skin and an altogether welcome lack of thinking. "You have my permission to do more than kissing."

Which he did, and it was glorious.

"This isn't going to end well, I can tell," he murmured, but he was picking her up as if she weighed nothing and carrying her out of the living area, through a hallway and then there was a door and an inviting lack of light from anything but the moon. And there was a bed. A big and beautiful bed with soft cotton sheets and many pillows and Max was there, shucking off his shoes and his watch and muttering something about sanity or lack of it and that just wasn't *on*, and she reached up and grabbed hold of his shirt front and dragged him back into her arms, where he belonged.

He got with the program remarkably swiftly after that, stripping her naked while she did the same for him, and he was enough to make her breath catch in her throat, and his lips on her breasts was enough to spin her out into orbit, and he was generous, too generous, with his attentions and she was altogether too grateful.

Lips and skin and clever, *clever* hands getting her ready for him and when he finally pressed into her she was already on the precipice and had been for a while. One thrust and a thoroughly possessive kiss tipped her over into ecstasy and he laughed as if she delighted him—and when had that ever happened for her during sex—and before she could follow that thought to any kind of conclusion, he kneeled up on the bed, bringing her with him and setting up a thoroughly delicious rhythm that she rewarded with gasping praise and possibly begging.

Definitely begging.

Right before he took his own release and she came for him again.

THE COMEDOWN WAS easier that she thought it would be, what with the warm sheets and the cover of darkness and the distinct lack of speaking. She lost herself in the examination of his face at rest. Eyes closed and those amazing lashes casting shadows any cinematographer would wax lyrical over. His mouth firm yet generous. His skin warm beneath her questing fingers as she closed her eyes and traced his cheek and committed the moment to memory.

"What are you doing?"

A worthy voice for a midnight tryst. The puff of his breath against her questing fingertips. "Braille."

"Pretty sure lips don't count as braille."

"Pretty sure your lips should count as something." She tucked into his side, her eyes still closed and shifted her hand to his chest and the steady up-down, up-down of it was more soothing than she would ever admit. "We should do that again."

His arm came up from underneath her shoulder as he drew her close and pressed his lips to her hair. "Glad to hear it. You staying the night or do you want me to drive you back?"

"I'm—" Currently undecided.

"Stay," he whispered. "I'd like you to."

She didn't always sleep well in new places. She liked her routines. She needed to know where everything was if a nightmare woke her, and that included knowing where *she* was the moment she opened her eyes. But he was so warm and alive beneath her touch and when he kissed her again, certain parts of him already hardening against her once more, she figured they might not do much sleeping anyway and that was a plan she could get behind.

She rolled over on top of him, enjoying the way his smile widened as she took his wrists and positioned them above his head. A smile like that demanded a kiss and she gave him one, and lingered because he was so damn good at this. "There are places I haven't kissed you yet. Must've missed them earlier. Here, for example." She tilted her head and put her lips to the underside of his jaw.

"I noticed that." There was a smile in his voice and surrender in his loins as he arched lazily beneath her. "City girl. Rush, rush, ru—oh dear God."

The man had very sensitive nipples. Begged the question what else might make a laid-back country boy acquire a sense of urgency. She badly wanted to find out. She sat up and undid the clip from the undoubtedly messy bun of her hair before lowering her hands to his waist and positioning his hardening length against the soft slickness of her folds. He really was ... incredibly ... ah ... responsive ... to her touch. It was very heady.

She lifted off him and scooted down and put her lips to his stomach, just below the cut of his hips and just to one side of his shaft, and licked. Kitten licks, a tease, nothing more.

So lovely, the way he squirmed.

"I could stay a while longer," she whispered, and slowly, diligently, with impeccable attention to detail, took him apart.

Chapter Six

IT WAS HER restlessness that woke him rather than her whimpering. The sudden jerk of her body towards the edge of the bed, hunching forward. The puff of her breath into the pillow beneath her head that shouldn't have been loud enough for him to hear, but he heard it nonetheless. Maggie remained still for just enough time for him to wonder whether gathering her close would be a good idea, and then her body jerked again.

"Mum."

He could barely hear her.

"Dad."

Oh, he heard that one all right. There was a sense of urgency to it that sent a shiver down his spine and he figured he knew exactly where she was in her dreams. He pulled her back against him, his arm around her waist and his body pressing against hers in a long, firm line. "Maggie, time to wake up."

But touch was no comfort to her, far from it, and she began to struggle in earnest. Against his arms. Locked in her dream.

"No. Oh, no. No. Wake up! Daddy!"

He'd heard those words before, years ago, and nothing good had ever come of them. "Maggie, it's me." He didn't want to go there. Didn't want to remember. "Maggie, c'mon."

Maggie you have to get out of the car, c'mon, let's go!

It was the voice of his younger self and he could hear the fear in it. "Maggie, *please*." Bad idea to pin her clawing hands to the bed when she wasn't awake, because her struggles increased and so did her panicked breathing and it was a mixture of *no* and *let me go*, infused with ascending degrees of terror.

"Let me go, let me go, they're still in there, you have to let me go."

"Maggie, you're dreaming."

"Let me go." As she fought to break free of his hold. "I hate you. How can you? *Let me go!*"

And this time he let her go.

He was out of the bed and across the room so fast he was dizzy from it, and he sagged against the door frame and ran his hand through his hair and watched in growing horror as she rode out her nightmare to its inevitable screaming conclusion and then sat bolt upright, eyes wide and gasping for breath and whether she saw him standing there was anyone's guess, but she scrunched her eyes tight again and began to speak again, even as she reached out for something to the right of the bed and didn't find it.

"One-one hundred, two-one hundred, it's okay Maggie, you're in your bed, three-one hundred ..." Fingers curling into the sheet beneath her. "Four-one hundred … You're right here." As she opened her eyes and stared straight at him and this time there was recognition there and sick realisation.

"Oh fuck," she said, and her knees came up and her arms wrapped around her legs. "I'm at your place."

"Yes." He was surprised he managed more than a rasp.

"In your bed."

"Yes."

"Right." And if there was an undercurrent of hysteria in there somewhere, well, maybe her nightmare hadn't quite left her yet. "I, ah, don't suppose I could have a glass of water?"

He could do that. And maybe some pyjama trousers from his cupboard on the way out. He made it to the living area before he stopped to put them on and then he went to the fridge and hung off the door like a guy coming off a three-day drunk and desperately in need of water. Icy air blasted over his skin, a match for the freeze that had taken him over at Maggie's sudden awakening. There was water in a bottle somewhere and he found it and then glasses and then he had to stand and breathe a while before continuing.

Maggie wanted water and he'd get it to her, he would. But maybe he needed to settle first.

He didn't get the chance.

She stood in the doorway, barefoot but clothed, her dress on and his white dinner shirt over it, buttoned to the collar and she was clutching it around her as if she thought he might wrest it from her, and he didn't know what it *meant* that she was wearing his shirt, but apparently her subconscious regularly screamed and fought and railed against him for something that had happened all those years ago when they were kids.

He poured, carefully, and slid the glass across the counter towards her, and she settled on a barstool and pulled it towards her but didn't lift it to her lips. The fingers of her right hand seemed to be silently playing the piano against the surface of the bench. She was still counting.

"How often do you have them?" he asked into the deafening silence, and watched as her fingers faltered.

"Nightmares?" She waited for his nod of confirmation. "Maybe once a week since I've been back here. I—I have routines that help. I can unravel pretty fast if I don't keep them."

"Is it always the same dream?"

She nodded. "I had one counsellor who wanted me to imagine a different ending, a happier ending, and that worked for a while—until she found out what that ending was."

He had no trouble imagining what that ending was. Maggie died with them. Blessed peace. "Where was I in your new ending?"

"Probably still practising rebellion down by the river," she said with a wry twist to her lips and finally picked up the water and drank. "Do you think—could we have some music?"

He reached for his phone and scrolled through until he

found a playlist he used in the shearing shed, hard edged and driving and leaning heavily on the songs of his teenage years. The press of a command had the sound issuing from speakers in the lounge area.

She gave a helpless little giggle that choked into nothing when he glared at her. Her imaginary piano playing started up again and he wondered if she started all over again with the counting when interrupted, or whether she picked up where she left off. *One-one hundred...*

"We should probably talk about this," she offered hesitantly.

You think? But he found he had absolutely nothing to say. "Or we could leave it alone. Let's do that." Because there really wasn't a lot he could say other than 'you still hate what I did all those years ago and if I had to do it all over again I wouldn't change a thing'. Or maybe he could go with 'I've never slept with a woman who has nightmares about me before and I'm pretty sure I never want to do it again'. "I need a little time with this, Maggie. Please."

"I know I talk in my sleep. If it was something I said—"

"You screamed. That's it. We're good."

"Oh," she said faintly and abandoned her finger tapping to clutch his shirt more tightly around her body. "Good." Her gaze flickered towards him and then away, as if it hurt to look at him. "That's good."

They were so far from good. "You want that lift home now?" He offered because his mother had raised him right and because he doubted he could stand there one more second without indulging in his own mental breakdown. "Or is there something else you'd like? Food? A shower?"

"I could head home." She nodded. "I could borrow your car and get someone else to drop it back late—

"No."

"—Because there's coffee there, you see, and a shower and seventy-four steps between my bedroom door and the kitchen light switch and it's the routine, you see. I like the routine."

"Collect your things, I'll take you home." No way could he watch her walk out that door with his car keys in hand, a subconscious death wish lodged in her head and no clear knowledge of how to get home. He was in over *his* head, no question, but he wasn't certifiable.

He drove her home, but he didn't make the mistake of putting his hands on her again. Instead, he stood by the car and waited while she picked her barefoot way across the gravel and climbed the three or four steps to the verandah. Dawn was breaking and he doubted either of them would be going back to bed.

She turned when she reached the top step, her eyes seeking out his. "Would you like a coffee?"

"Maybe another time."

She squared her shoulders. "Of course. Thank you for the lift. And the ... rest." She didn't wait for his reply, which was good, because he didn't have one. She went inside. He left.

He'd been so insistent on Maggie taking her time when

it came to deciding what to do with her inheritance. He'd coerced her into staying because he'd been of the opinion that it'd be good for her to confront the ghosts of her past. A big part of him had wanted her to stay on and build a life with *him*. Nowhere in his reckoning did he account for the trauma her subconscious might serve up every time she fell asleep. He'd been of the decidedly idiotic opinion that they could lay their past to rest.

More fool him.

A rational man whose heart was still his own would take one look at the danger to his sanity and hers and back right off. A rational person would not consider turning around a dozen times during the drive home, or sending someone over to make sure she was all right, one-one hundred fucking two-one hundred and counting.

A rational person wouldn't stand beneath the shower thirty minutes later and put his palms to the tiles and his face to the spray and sob for futures lost.

Or maybe they would.

Chapter Seven

IN THE DAYS that followed her ill-fated evening with Max, Maggie gave working herself to distraction her best shot. She became fixated with the procuring of kitchen appliances. She took possession of an antique dining table for the ballroom. It fit together in pieces and could seat one hundred people once all the sections were in place. One hundred people in splendour, or one hundred and twenty at a pinch, and *of course* she had to order stainless steel cutlery and table napkins for it, and glassware and bowls and plates. She finalised plans for a charity ball that would take place on the last day of summer and then recklessly went ahead and offered to host a long-table dinner for a hundred friends of the rural fire brigade in the hours beforehand.

She slept a sketchy two hours a night and the shadows beneath her eyes grew resistant to concealer, but she was keeping busy, getting by, determinedly *not* thinking about Max's smiles and Max's kisses and the ecstasy she'd found in his arms.

Not to mention the nightmare that had come afterwards.

She tried to remember what she might have said to put that look on Max's face as he'd stared at her from the shadows of the other side of the room. In her head it was usually some version of *no* or *let me go*, but she hadn't until three days ago realised that she might be saying some of it aloud.

He'd said not, but he'd looked shattered and he hadn't called her since. If that wasn't a big fat sign of having second thoughts about continuing a relationship with her, she didn't know what was.

She'd gone to dinner *expecting* his withdrawal once she told him about her medical history and the complexities involved when it came to her and motherhood. That hadn't put him off the way she thought it would and she'd been a whole lot too enamoured of that fact. She hadn't known what she wanted from him, but she'd invited herself over to his place, and …

Stop *lying*!

She'd known exactly what she'd wanted from him. She just hadn't realised how quickly it would drive him away. Who'd have thought that all she had to do to accomplish that was fall asleep in his presence?

The tight ball of misery in her chest would go away soon enough. The shame of not being good enough, or stable enough, or low maintenance enough would leave and instead she'd feel relief that Max knew his limits when it came to the for-better-or-for-worse parts of a relationship equation. And it hadn't taken him long to reach them.

It wasn't the worst thing that had ever happened to her, not by a long shot.

And then Max's mother turned up at Wirra homestead unannounced.

If Maggie had to describe Max's mother, elegant would have been the first word that came to mind and composed would have been the second. Eleanor O'Connor was an active member of the community and her sponge cakes were the stuff of legend. She'd always been pleasant but not overly effusive towards Maggie and Maggie had always been that little bit in awe of the woman.

There was no clear reason for her to be visiting.

"Mrs O'Connor, come in. I, er, would you like a tour? I've been meaning to—or tea, would you like tea? Or coffee?" The afternoon tea cakes were long gone and it wasn't as if she didn't order double the amount for her work crew to begin with. Wirra Station welcome and hospitality was starting all over again from the ground up and Maggie liked to think her workers took better care of the old homestead because of it. "I have biscuits—packet biscuits, but they do involve chocolate."

"Tea, thank you Margaret. Hold the biscuits for now and I'll take the tour later."

Which begged the question of where to put Max's mother while Maggie made the tea. Good manners suggested that the kitchen table wasn't the place to be herding visitors towards. "There's a sitting room down that way we could use. Or we could sit on the verandah overlooking the garden. It's looking very nice for this time of year, even with the heat and the lack of rain ..." And what was she *thinking* spouting weather conditions to a woman who'd lived here all her life?

"What's wrong with the kitchen?"

"It's not exactly finished." Maggie had extended it, and the builders had been busy installing cupboards and long benches and a bank of commercial fridges in the space. "And it's a little bit different now to what you might be expecting ... Oh, here we are, well, you can see for yourself what's happening in here. Coffee? No, no, it was tea."

The making of tea gave Maggie something to do and time to gather her thoughts. Would Max have told her what happened the other night? The thought was enough to turn her stomach. "What brings you here? Not that you're not welcome," she added hastily. "Because you are, of course—as a neighbour and Max's mother and a friend of Carmel's."

"Shall I get straight to the point?"

Oh, that sounded bad. "Sure."

"Your great-aunt left some matters with me for safekeeping. A box of papers and the like, with instructions to share them with you only if you decided to keep Wirra Station and live here. If you didn't I was to deliver the box to Carmel's solicitor."

Not what she'd been expecting. For starters, there was no Max in it. "Oh. I see. Do you have any idea what kind of papers are in the box?"

"Mainly some personal letters that she didn't want falling into outside hands. Explanations. Reasons for why she did the things she did. Things she never told you. She wasn't the best communicator, your great-aunt."

Eleanor O'Connor had a way with understatement. "I don't see any box."

"That's because it's at home. I spoke with Max this morning about your plans to stay on and his offer to buy, and he had no answer to give." Eleanor eyed her steadily. "Of course, he looked like he hadn't slept for a week and you don't look much better, so perhaps my timing is off. I'd been given to understand that your dinner meeting the other night would provide some clarity when it came to the future of Wirra Station."

There was blunt and then there was this. But Maggie could be blunt too, when she needed to be. "I'm trying to split the title—as I'm sure you know. My petition is currently with the heritage council and if I get permission to do so I've already agreed to sell the land portion to Max. I'm not sure where that leaves your box."

"What happens if you're unsuccessful?"

"Then I'm going to have a lot of prime grazing land I don't know what to do with." *And a mountain of debt on account of all the money she was spending on the homestead.* "My business acumen might not be up to the task of making a go of a function centre and wedding venue business on a shoestring budget. I might sell the lot and move on. Max has already expressed his willingness to buy Wirra Station outright."

"At a price I consider ridiculous."

"At a price that will be renegotiated between Max and myself, taking into account monies spent. Mrs O'Connor, I don't know what you *want*. If it's guarantees, you're fresh out of luck. Life doesn't work like that. I don't know if I'm staying, because I don't know if I can make a go of this place or not. Carmel couldn't, and she'd lived here all her life."

"Not all her life." Eleanor's eyes narrowed as she sipped her tea. "Carmel's heart wasn't in it."

"And yet she stayed to the very end. Have you any idea how often I asked her to come and live with me? Hell, I couldn't even get her to come and stay with me for a weekend!"

"She was also very stubborn. Didn't like being wrong."

A comment that drew a brief bark of laughter from Maggie. "Who does?"

"Indeed. No-one likes being wrong. I never thought you'd return, yet here you are, and you and Max are the talk of the town. Again."

Oh, this was going so well. "I've never been able to regulate what other people say about me. Half of them make it up as they go. And although I'm working hard to become a part of this community in a way I never have been before, I don't know how to fix the gossip. I'm trying to ignore it."

Her words seemed to set Max's mother back a step, but not for long. "I have to confess, I too have been guilty of speculating about you over the years. Carmel and I often talked about the possibility of you and my son getting together. You seemed oddly drawn to one another as children and young adults. Carmel thought it a result of Max being there for you the night your parents died. And while I always gave that argument credit, I often thought there was a little more to it than that."

And wasn't *that* a conversation Maggie didn't want to have. "Max is an extraordinary man. He was an extraordinary boy and I have nothing but praise for him. But I don't see us getting together romantically."

"Is that because you'll find it difficult to have children?"

Maggie sat back, stung. "Max *told* you that?"

"No, Max never mentioned it and I doubt he ever will. Carmel needed a sounding board when you were first injured and I was there for her—already involved through Max in a way that others weren't. I was there with her at the hospital the day the doctors wanted to remove your reproductive system, but Carmel wasn't having it. Only one of your ovaries was damaged beyond repair and she saw absolutely no reason for the other one to be removed. She told them that if you came out of surgery with both of them gone she'd sue every last person in the room and the hospital too. Your great-aunt could be intimidating when she wanted to be."

And at all other times too.

Max's mother lowered her tea cup to the saucer with careful deliberation. "I didn't know if she was doing the right thing by you, no-one did, but they left it in. Then she refused to give you the hormone treatments they wanted you to have. I argued against her on that one. I thought perhaps you needed the hormone treatment. Carmel obsessed for years over your height and weight. You were so small and slight and for years you barely grew. Turns out she was right to protect you from additional hormones back then, if recent findings are true."

Maggie didn't care for being discussed behind her back, or told of it years later. "My health, or lack of it, can surely be of no interest to you."

"It is if you're looking to be romantically involved with my son. One of the reasons I came here was to reassure you that if Max brings you into our family you will have our complete support when it comes to what you will or won't do about having children."

"Even if I'd rather remain childless?"

"Even then."

"I don't believe you. Farming dynasties need heirs."

"So they do. And yet people have a distressing tendency to love as they will and damn the consequences." Max's mother stood and offered her a tight smile. "You're a lot like her, you know. Prickly. Hard to decipher. Drive someone away before they get close enough to hurt you. I have one child and one child only and his happiness means the world to me. Make him happy and you'll make me happy. Maybe that you can believe. Having said that, I know when Max is hurting and if you *ever* blame him again for pulling you out of that wreck I'm going to crush your grand business plans to dust and then drive you out of the district."

Maggie blinked. "I ... see? But here's the thing. I don't blame your son for saving my life. That would be ridiculous, and unfair, and maybe when it *happened* I would have given anything to free my parents as well, but that didn't happen, obviously, and it was no-one's fault. Obviously."

"Tell him that."

"I ... Do you think I need to? Doesn't he know?"

The older woman's hard gaze softened, just a little. "I think he could stand to hear it again. Especially from you."

Oh, Lord. Did this have something to do with her nightmare the other night? What exactly had she said in her sleep? "I'll speak to him," she offered in all sincerity. "He shouldn't be thinking that."

"There is one more thing before I go."

"Really?" Because what with the box conversation and the contemplation of absent reproductive organs, and then the Max discussion, she was rather dreading what might come next. Maggie was a peaceable person at heart. She needed prior notice of impending conflict so she could armour-up. "Mrs O'Connor—"

"Eleanor."

Yeah, no. "Mrs O'Connor, I have an online meeting with suppliers in a couple of minutes." Couple of minutes, half an hour, same thing.

"This will only take a minute. Come with me. I need to see your great-aunt's room."

She knew the way and her stride was long. Maggie didn't exactly have to skip to keep up, but it was close.

"I like what you've done with the place," Eleanor O'Connor said, casually offhand. "Ah, here we are." She walked into Carmel's bedroom, which had been stripped of all personal belongings and now contained a bed, an ornate full-length mirror and a chaise lounge that had had the good fortune to have been reupholstered in soothing sage green. Max's mother walked through the room and into the walk-in robe area. This part of the room was scheduled for a refit and repaint but it hadn't happened yet and, in spite of it being empty, it still smelled ever so slightly of old clothes and shoes. Max's mother opened the top drawer of a stack of built-in drawers, but it was empty.

"There's nothing left in here," Maggie felt compelled to say. "Everything's been sorted and labelled, and I know where everything's gone, so if you tell me what you're looking for—"

Max's mother stuck her hand inside the drawer, palm up, and appeared to be reaching for something. There was a click; not the click of a shutting door but similar, deeper. Max's mother then stepped in behind the clothes rail, ducking her head as she did so, and put her back to the wall and pushed. The entire wall swung open to reveal some kind of storage room, dark and musty.

"There never was a light in here so don't bother looking for one," Max's mother said.

"I guess that would explain why the electricians didn't notice this when they redid the wiring. What is this place?"

"It's a wardrobe extension. Like I said, your aunt was a very private woman. There was a lot she didn't show. Now, if you'll excuse me, I'll leave you to get on with your day."

"Wait, you're leaving?"

"I've done all I came here to do. Why would I stay?"

"True. Don't let me keep you. I, um, thank you. I think." The older woman turned to leave and as much as Maggie longed to leave it at that, she couldn't. The box could wait. The hidden wardrobe could wait. What Eleanor O'Connor had said about Max needing to hear that Maggie didn't blame him for saving her … that couldn't wait. "Mrs O'Connor, where might I find Max today?"

"He's gone to NSW to look at a thousand head of sheep. We don't often buy out of state, but it's not often a superfine merino wool grower puts his breeding herd up for tender, either."

"And when will he be back?"

"Sometime today."

"Thanks. I'll catch up with him. So about these sheep? Do you have the room for them?"

"Not on a permanent basis, no. But you do."

✸

MAX'S FAMED EASYGOING friendliness had deserted him. Not even a six-hour drive and a decent meal at the end of it could pull him from his sour mood. He'd thought a break would do him good, that it wouldn't hurt to put some distance between himself and a certain doe-eyed seductress who could render a man boneless with pleasure and then slay him in her sleep.

Problem was, distance did nothing to alter that fact that he couldn't stop thinking about the utter rightness he'd felt as he'd held Maggie in his arms. In that moment he'd found what he'd been looking for all along. As if he'd finally come home.

And then the windows had cracked and the roof had fallen in and Maggie had reached out to him, shaken and so obviously damaged, and he'd been too shattered to reach back. All he'd done was stand there and stare, and then avoid her for the next three days, or four.

As if that was going to fix things.

He'd researched PTSD symptoms and coping strategies. He'd read a book on how to interpret nightmares. He had a meeting with a retiring wool grower in two hours' time, a grazier who had a century-old breeding program that he wanted to sell into safe hands—and Max was that person, his credentials spoke for him—but he shouldn't have come all this way without securing ownership or leasehold of Wirra Station land first, and he didn't have it. He needed answers, not more sheep, and he should have called Maggie days ago and tried to mend bridges, but he hadn't. He'd ordered a book on coping with childhood trauma instead.

And then his phone rang and it was Maggie and he manfully goddamn hesitated before taking the call. What was *wrong* with him?

"Hey." He aimed for jovial and missed it by a continent. "I'm glad you called."

"Have I caught you at a bad time?"

"No, just about to go and look at some sheep."

"So your mother said."

His mother? What was his mother doing getting in Maggie's ear? Because he'd spoken with his mother this morning and he hadn't particularly liked the direction her questions had been going. "She's there with you?"

"She was earlier. She came around to show me a secret closet in Carmel's bedroom."

"You have a secret closet now?"

"Yep."

"What's in it?"

"Memories. Clothes, even a wedding gown, along with a photograph of a fiancé who died in a war, and a safe I don't have the combination for. Did I mention that your mother has this box that belonged to Carmel and I'm not allowed to have it unless I decide to stay here and I don't know whether I'm staying or not, and I know I said something to you in my sleep the other night, but I don't know what, and you don't think I blame you for my parents' deaths, do you? Or for saving me? Because that would be dumb."

Max stared at the top shelf offerings of the pub bar and wondered whether he could get the barman to drag down the bottle of Laphroaig single malt and just keep pouring. "You want to run through all that again? A little slower this time?"

"Not really. Not all of it's important. Most of it was a lead-in to asking what I did or said the other night to put you off. Because there has to be some reason you're avoiding me and I refuse to believe you're the type of man to bed a woman and then drop her without a word."

"I could be that kind of man." Which was worse? Letting

her think that or admitting that as much as he wanted her, he wasn't at all sure that she wanted him? "How do you know I'm not?"

"Instinct. Apart from that, you're not stupid enough to jeopardise your purchase of Wirra Station by acting like an arsehole."

"I might be that stupid." He *had* been that stupid.

"Three nights ago I went to sleep thinking there was nowhere else I'd rather be, and when I woke up—granted, in a bit of a state—things had changed. I have some PTSD symptoms I probably should have mentioned, and, yes, that could be more than enough reason to give you pause. But then this morning your mother warned me not to hurt you again. I don't want to jump to any conclusions, but I'm really beginning to think I might have. So if you could just tell me what I did, I'd really like to fix it. Even if it's only fixable to the point where we're on casually friendly terms again."

"Or we could drop it."

"You said that the other night, but I don't think that approach is working for us."

She did have a point. "I woke up to find you struggling in my arms and I tried to soothe you, but you wouldn't wake up. You demanded I let you go. So I did."

Silence.

He could leave it at that, but she'd asked him for honesty and maybe it would explain his retreat in the way other words never could. "You told me you hated me. And then you woke up. And I don't know where to go from there when it comes to you and me, Maggie. I really don't."

"I don't hate you. I never have." She sounded so earnest.

"Your subconscious does."

"My subconscious thinks I should have died trying to save my parents—doesn't mean I agree with it." She sounded altogether too close to tears for comfort. "I'm sorry I spooked you. But I need you to know that I don't have a death wish and I certainly don't hate you. I never have. You're the finest person I know. You saved my life."

And it was still haunting them both.

"Was the sex so terrible?" she asked quietly.

"You know it wasn't." He'd never had better.

"Then we could do it again. And not sleep afterwards and maybe we could just kind of ease into things a little more slowly. Maybe that'd work."

He waited too long to reply and she haltingly filled the gap.

"Or not. Just a thought. I'm very aware relationships shouldn't be this hard, what with the nightmares and the fertility challenges and I'm just going to hang up now, okay? And chalk it up to experience. But I don't hate you, that's the take home and I really hope you believe me. Never that."

She made him feel so small. He'd never thought of himself as a coward before. "I suppose we could ease our way up to slumber parties," he offered gruffly. "We could do that."

"You could start by coming around to see the cupboard the universe has seen fit to unveil. We could stare at the safe

I can't open and take guesses as to what's in it. We could do this while drinking wine from the cellar and suggesting combinations. There's a riveting date for you."

"I'll bring popcorn." He was trying. They both were. And he felt better for it than he'd felt in three days.

Silence fell, a little awkward, a little sweet.

"I'm really sorry about what happened the other night," she muttered. "I never want to hurt you. Please believe that."

"You didn't."

"Yes," she said. "I did."

Chapter Eight

MAX BOUGHT POPPING corn and butter from the supermarket on the way back through Wirralong later that afternoon. He thought about bringing flowers, but the simple fact was that the flowers from Maggie's garden would put store-bought offerings to shame. He bought cheeses and crackers, because adding wine and a cheese platter to a night spent staring at a safe seemed like a good thing to do. Then he added hot chocolate powder and marshmallows in case he was on the wrong track altogether. He'd bought a thousand sheep today, with no clear idea yet of where he was going to put them. His judgement wasn't exactly sound.

The smile Maggie gave him when he arrived at the homestead, shopping bag in one hand and an electric torch with an extension cord in the other, could have lit the dark side of the moon.

"I knew you'd be a useful person to know," she told him, and before he knew it they were sitting down to warm roast beef rolls and he was staring around with frank amazement at the pictures of Carmel Walker on the walls of a long, narrow dressing room.

"You said hidden closet," he managed, between mouthfuls. "You could fit a bed in here. I think this qualifies as a hidden room." He stared at the ancient wall safe the size of a small drawer. "Know any safecrackers?"

"Not a one. Do you?" She was a woman who could set a picnic table that included a bowl of marshmallows, a mason jar full of jelly babies and his favourite type of mustard—and pair it all with fine linen napkins, cut-crystal wine glasses and a bottle of red wine older than he was.

"No. You've tried every date of birth in your family tree?"

"And date of death."

"Don't be morbid."

"I'm sitting here surrounded by a champagne-coloured wedding dress, three chinchilla fur coats, an emu-feathered vest and a signed picture of Elvis. I'm allowed to be a little bit morbid," she countered and maybe she was right.

"Have you tried Wirra Station's latitude and longitude?"

"Well I would if I knew what it was."

He rattled off numbers and she spun the dial, but no joy. They tried acreage next, then hectares, then random knob twirling while listening for a click, but neither of them had a stethoscope and that only worked in the movies anyway. They worked their way through the meal and the wine— there was an art to decanting it—and tried Elvis's birth date. And then Elvis's date of death while munching on a jelly baby.

"No, no. We're getting the dates wrong for Elvis," she

said. "Month comes before day in the US."

So they tried it again.

And it opened.

"Huh." she said, staring at the open safe in amazement. "How about that?"

It was at that point Max swore undying devotion to Maggie Walker, she of the messy bun, doe-brown eyes and weakness for all the yellow jelly babies with extra white stuff on them.

"Well?" Not that he was impatient. "Is it full of hundred-dollar notes?"

"Nope. It's full of boxes." She pulled one out and handed it to him and withdrew a far smaller ring box for herself. "What's the bet this is the engagement ring?"

"Wouldn't she have worn it?"

"Oh, this is pretty."

He leaned over her shoulder to have a look. A ring was a ring was a ring, but this one screamed money and class. Not too big, not too small and even beneath makeshift light it glittered. "Is it an engagement ring?"

"I don't know. Could be, but I'm not really feeling it as an engagement ring. It's more of a dress ring. Now open yours."

"It's like Christmas, only not." His box contained a watch with a brand name he'd heard of, but never seen in the wild. "I think your money situation is about to take a turn for the better."

"It's just a watch."

She leaned forward to look more closely at the timepiece and the temptation to do the same was overwhelming. The closer he got to this woman the harder he fell, and he didn't know why except that there was something about her hard-won resilience that called to him. She'd seen the black, and it haunted her still, but she always got back up again and maybe this time the universe was helping. "It's vintage Patek Philippe with barely a mark on it. It's a collector's watch and worth more than you think." He closed the lid and gently set it away from the food. The watch was a beauty, but he had something to get off his chest. "I'm sorry I walked away from you the other night. I shouldn't have."

"Why not?" She smiled and didn't look away from him. "You were protecting yourself. There's no shame in that."

"I shouldn't have done it. I should have seen to you."

She put her palm to his cheek and kissed him gently on the lips. "You're here aren't you? You came back. It's up to me now to treat you right." She pulled back, her eyes bright and dug back into the bowels of the safe. "Let's see what else we've got."

A tennis bracelet to match the diamond and emerald ring. Some old coins. An antique opal brooch. A pocket watch. *Another* men's watch, this one a Vacheron Constantin.

"Not to alarm you, but there's a reason these watches were so well hidden," he said with a frown. "They're worth a fortune."

"Then why didn't Carmel sell them when she needed the

money?"

"Maybe her decision to let Wirra Station run down wasn't about the money. Maybe it was her version of retirement."

"She never talked about family with me. Not family history, not her life beyond Wirra Station. She once said her father was a bastard. That's it. She never said a word about any of this." Maggie slumped back against the wall and took a deep breath. "Problem is, my workers know this room is here now. The secret is out. I even put pictures up on the blog, which in hindsight may not have been altogether smart of me. Are these watches and things too valuable to keep here now?"

"Yes."

"Do *you* have a safe?"

"Yes, and *hell no* to putting these in mine. I suggest we take a drive to Melbourne tomorrow. You need bank security for these."

"You could stay the night and offer to protect them," she murmured, as she handed him a jelly baby and a grape. "I could offer incentive. Another bottle of wine."

"Maggie Walker, you opportunistic devil." He liked her playful and relaxed. He liked the way she gave melancholy its due as she paused to consider each item before putting them back in the safe. He didn't think she saw dollar signs or status symbols when she looked at the things Carmel had treasured.

"I want to make a toast," she said, and raised her glass to

a picture of the woman who'd barely given her the time of day. "To Carmel and her secrets. May she rest in peace."

To Carmel.

There was more wine. More food. Laughter and then he reached out to take some of the hair falling over her shoulder between his fingertips. It felt like silk against his calluses and he couldn't resist giving it a tiny tug. He'd always craved her attention and now he had it. "How slow do you think we need to go when it comes to getting undressed again?"

"Not that slow," she whispered against his lips.

There were kisses in the hidden closet room, more kisses in the bedroom and then breath-stealing intimacy on the bed. Max let himself feel rather than think, gave himself over to Maggie's touch and allowed himself to possess that which he'd always coveted. He could lose himself in this woman and he did.

Later, much later, Maggie set him up with a glass of water on the bedside table and a towel on the end of the bed. She showed him where the new bathroom was and where her room was and told him he could stay over and claim any of the other bedrooms as his. He offered to stay in Carmel's room, the one they'd just used, and she walked him back there and hovered uncertainly in the doorway.

"So, I'll see you in the morning?" she said.

He knew what she was saying. "If you're up at six you will. I'll be the one hovering over your coffee machine, willing it to work."

"I'll see you in the morning, then." She looked relieved.

"Good night."

"Sleep well." He kissed her again and then watched her leave.

If this was how it worked for them, then this was how it worked.

※

THE NEXT TWO weeks were a study in pleasure for Maggie. During the day she worked to pull her vision for Wirra homestead together, revelling in the way the old house began to warm and glow beneath her ministrations, its majestic beauty revealed now that the years of neglect had been scrubbed away. During the night, she lost herself in Max's arms for hours at a time. He took over the master bedroom, declaring it his kind of room, and there were nights when it was enough to lie in his arms and feel the warmth of his skin against hers and the solid thud of his heart against her hand.

She never slept in his presence, that was her rule. She was too fearful of bad dreams that she couldn't control. Instead, she'd stay for as long as she could, until sleep threatened to drag her under, and then she'd slip from his bed and go find her own. He always woke long enough to kiss her and tell her to get some sleep.

Some days he insisted she go with him to shift sheep or evaluate pasture growth, slowly introducing her to farming decisions and options for the land she now owned. He did his best to interest her in the work that he loved, and it *was* interesting, and her respect for the business he'd built grew. He had time for people—that was his secret weapon—and a confidence that came from deep within. The only person who could shake his solid belief in himself was her—or so it seemed—and she didn't do it deliberately.

There was still no word on whether or not she could subdivide the land—the promised three-day time frame for a reply had come to nothing. Meanwhile her conservation management plan for the homestead had been fast-tracked and approved. Yes, Jeannie Lamb and her husband Ron had been a godsend when it came to dealing with the state's heritage laws. Yes, she could spend outrageous sums of money in an effort to comply with their rules. She celebrated the win with her once-a-month Monday night ladies, who never failed to make her feel good about what she was doing.

Wirra Station was beginning to feel like home, and it was a beautiful home full of rich history and little things that delighted her.

She quietly lowered the sale price on her Melbourne home and prayed that it would sell. She made discreet inquiries about vintage watch dealers who specialised in buying and selling high-end pieces. Home repair continued at a more leisurely pace now that all the major work had been done. There was an end of summer finish date to coincide with the ball.

And then Max casually mentioned that he was due in Italy at the end of the month and wouldn't be around for the ball after all and the sheer weight of her disappointment blindsided her, even as she made the morning coffee and made small talk as if there was nothing wrong.

He picked up on it, though. He always did. "These meetings have been scheduled for months," he said. "And the relationships I have with these buyers and processors means that they want to see *me*, the boss man, not someone else. I can't delegate this."

"You have to go, I get that. There'll be other balls here, that's the plan." She turned and fixed him with a smile. "Of course, this one may well be a spectacular failure, spoken about with reverence for years to come, and then you'll be sorry you missed it."

"It won't be a failure, it'll be a spectacular success and I'm already sorry I'm missing it."

He sounded sincere and she had no reason to doubt him. *She* was the insecure one here, reading more into his absence than she should. "Your belief in my vision is most welcome," she said ruefully, and planted a kiss on his temple. "Even if I am going to curse your name as I panic my way towards the speeches part of the evening. Who's going to make fun of me and tell me I can do this? Who's going to know what to do when the Castle family and the Montgomery clan realise their respective son and daughter are conducting a secret romance worthy of Romeo and Juliet, thus ending a hundred years of feuding? And that they got together while working for me at the homestead?"

"Ma Castle already knows. Nothing gets past that woman. And her silence is consent."

"See? How do you know this and I don't?"

"I'm networked. You'll get there."

She harrumphed him. He grinned, and it occurred to her that she was in love with him. Not in a *let's make do* kind of way. Not in a *this is convenient and why not* kind of way. It was more of a soul deep realisation that his was the face she wanted to see first thing every morning and the last thing every night. It was quite the realisation to be having at six am on a workday morning.

"I'm going to miss you," she said. "People are going to think I'm in the market for romance and I'm not going to be able to say *oh look, there's Max*."

"You underestimate the Wirralong grapevine. People know we're together."

"They do?" Sure, her employees knew he stayed over on a regular basis, but they also knew he had his own room and it wasn't just for appearances' sake. All the Henderson contractors who set foot on the place knew they answered to him rather than Maggie, but that could be explained by a business arrangement between two adjoining landholders. Or Max simply being helpful while she found her feet. "Are you sure?"

"Want me to kiss you in the main street before I leave?"

"Yes." Yes, she did. "Don't you grin at me. I'm a needy woman who craves acceptance and if I have to use you to get it, I'll do it."

"Oh, that's cold." He finished his coffee and put the mug in the dishwasher, a clear signal that he was getting ready to leave. "Wednesday at noon in front of the post office. I'll be there. The question is, will you?"

✷

MAGGIE AND MAX'S warm yet restrained public kiss took place as scheduled, but the gossip that followed took a slightly unexpected turn, according to Elsa. And if you couldn't trust your hairdresser to know all the best rumours in town, who could you trust?

"Max, you'll be pleased to know your mystique is alive and well, regardless of our current dating status," she told him two days later as she sat on a steel rail overlooking a sheep pen. The yards were connected to his woolshed and Max was wedged somewhere in the middle of said pen, opening mouths and looking at teeth and occasionally lifting an animal into the adjacent pen. "You do realise the health and safety police would have a field day with you doing that?"

"Uh huh." He really wasn't listening, so she leaned forward to pat the nearest woolly head and lo, his oversize collared shirt slid straight off her shoulder.

She wasn't wearing anything beneath it.

He looked up and his smile grew downright wicked and she preened ever so slightly beneath his attention. She loved appropriating his clothing every so often and then showing up clad in it. It made his already glorious blue eyes darken possessively and she could practically guarantee that at some point during the day he would take his shirt back. It was as good as a painted sign on her forehead that said 'take me to bed, right now, this minute'.

"Something you want me to do for you?" Seriously, no other bedroom voice compared to his.

"Yes, I want you to listen to me. The town grapevine has decided you're harbouring a secret love for another man ... an Italian fashion designer who keeps sending you the most amazing clothes to wear. I'm your beard."

His eyes narrowed and the sea of wool parted effortlessly for him as he stalked towards her. "You're my *beard* now?" His hands landed on either side of her on the rail, effectively caging her in.

"That's what they say. I've been defeated by your love of good tailoring and a foreign accent."

"Because *I* have it on good authority that you have me twisted around your little finger."

"Oh, really?" She liked the sound of that. "Hadn't heard that one."

"That's because my workforce is loyal only to me and they refrain from making their observations known while in your presence."

"You could always refute their wild claims."

"I tried. Problem is, it's true. You do have me wrapped around your little finger." He nuzzled in, his lips tracking the sweetest path across her neck and cheek before finally claiming a kiss and Maggie lost track of time and the world around them and only the sharp whistle of someone calling for attention brought her back to earth.

"Oy, boss! Where do you want these sheep?"

One of Max's younger farmhands was standing in the doorway, hands on hips and his smirk barely hidden beneath the brim of his dusty brown hat. Two dogs stood beside him, tongues lolling.

"Were you supposed to be opening a gate for that man?" she murmured, leaning in close and using Max's body as a shield as she straightened her shirt.

"I do believe I was."

"Then you'd best go do it."

"I'm in the middle of something." He raised his voice and turned his head, still shielding her. "Put them in the south-side run."

"I'll go get the gate for him." She swung her legs over the pen and slid nimbly to the ground, buttons buttoned and her hair, well, her hair might be a little mussed.

"Helpful."

"I try."

"Or I could keep you right here with me. Do you even know which gate to open?"

"We put sheep in there last week." She offered up a smile as she backed away, still facing him, not quite ready to stop teasing him. "I may only be your beard but I do make a point of paying attention when you show me things."

"I like that about you."

"And what are your thoughts on the beard gossip?"

"Adds to my mystique." He nodded sagely. "You realise I

have no idea where I'm up to with this pen of sheep and now I have to start again?"

"Enjoy. I'm heading back to the homestead anyway, to take delivery of gauze curtains." She sniffed at the arm of her shirt. "I may have to change first. Do I smell of you?"

"Yes." Smug satisfaction looked good on him. "And I smell of sheep."

✸

"I'M HAVING A summer romance," Maggie told her friend during a phone call two days later. She'd been wanting to get Isabella Martenson to visit her for ages, not least because Izzy was a marriage celebrant who could—given the right incentive—play an integral part in Maggie's destination wedding business plans. They'd forged a solid friendship during their mutual time in Melbourne and, of everyone she'd left behind, Maggie missed Isabella the most. Their friendship wasn't a minefield of differing values or opinions. Friendship with Izzy was just plain *easy*. "I also have a spare ticket to a charity dinner and ball I'm giving in a couple of weeks' time, courtesy of my summer romance deserting me in favour of meeting up with a handsome fashion designer in Italy. Would you like to come? Could you spare the time? Because I also want to talk business with you."

"When's it on?"

"Last Saturday in February. I know you probably have a wedding booked in for that Saturday, because who doesn't want to get married on the last Saturday in summer—unless it's bad luck. Is it bad luck?"

"It must be." Izzy sounded distracted. "The couple I was supposed to be marrying on that day cancelled on me last week."

"So you *can* come?"

"I'm not sure. I still have one wedding ceremony to officiate on the Sunday and it's a little late to tell the bride and groom I want to tap out and get someone else to marry them. On the other hand, I do know someone who might do it. I miss you. I want invitations to these things up front and preferably six months out. And if you could make them on a Monday I'd appreciate it, because that's my day off. But, hey. No pressure."

"There's an occasional Monday gathering here that I think you'd like. It's full of smart ladies who want to make something of themselves and the opportunities that come their way. Champagne and big ideas are often involved."

"I like the sound of that. Tell me more about this ball. What's it for?"

"The ticket says all proceeds will be going to the rural fire brigade service, and that part's true. But it's also a way for me to reach out to the residents of Wirralong, which is the little town nearby, and get them on board with what I'm trying to create out here. It's going to be an absolutely fabulous evening but, fair warning, it'll be my first time using a local chef and half the catering team is more used to outside work than carrying a dinner plate. We're having two training runs beforehand for the waitstaff, but this is a trial-by-fire event for all concerned, including me. Your job, should you choose to accept it, is to peel me off the wall and potentially keep me away from the wine, if things go badly—at least until everybody else leaves."

"Wow, you're really selling it," Izzy said dryly.

"Did I mention it's for the rural fire brigade service? And that I'm hoping to get some promo pics out of it? And that there's a room here with your name on it? Actually, there's a little sandstone cottage here with your name on it, and I want to talk to you about that at some point, because I have an idea. I'm also dying to show you the homestead. Iz, it *welcomes*. I want you to see it. I know this isn't the first time I've asked you, but it's the first time I truly need a friend here in my corner. Can you get someone to cover your Sunday bookings? Come for the weekend. Come for the week."

"You really need me there?"

"I really do. I'm trying not to fret about having to be a vivacious and confident hostess, but you know me. I'm just as likely to revert to type and go hide in a cupboard. Did I mention the rural fire brigade connection?"

"Three times so far. Wouldn't want to disappoint the rural fire brigade."

"So you'll be here?"

"I will."

"I love you. I *owe* you."

"Good. Now tell me about your summer romance."

There was no getting around it. "Have I ever mentioned Max to you?"

"As in farm boy Max with the blue eyes and the unruly hair and the long, long legs? Max the saviour and bane of your existence from school years seven to eleven?"

"So I have mentioned him."

Isabella laughed. "Yes, darling heart. You have. Why is he only yours for the summer?"

"Oh, you know."

"I know nothing of the sort. Why don't you keep him?"

"He might not want to be kept by me. I can be a little high maintenance."

"Who told you that? Does this have anything to do with Richard the Jerk?"

"It doesn't."

"It better not."

She'd missed this friendship. Izzy's fierce loyalty. "Thank you for coming to Wirra homestead's first ever ball. You won't regret it."

"Maggie." Izzy's voice was rich with affection. "It's going to be so good to see you again. I've missed you lots. You know that if you ever need me to be somewhere, all you ever have to do is ask."

✸

THE NEXT TWO weeks were frantically busy. Maggie always had been a compulsive list maker and detail checker, and making sure the homestead was ready for an onslaught of guests fed her compulsion to the point of anxiety. It didn't help that Max left four days before the ball and that his absence brought home exactly how much she'd come to rely on his steady presence and calming influence. He really did seem to bring out the best in her. It scared her, just a little, to think that she couldn't do this without him. That she'd tapped into his strength and not her own, and if that was the case then maybe his being away was a good thing. Maybe she did need to do this on her own in order to prove to herself and the wider community that she could.

She'd made love to Max the night before he'd left and, like always, she'd put her whole heart into it. She'd stayed too long afterwards, spooned naked in his arms and tried to stay awake, just doze, but she'd been so damn *tired* from all the work and she'd been so warm in the circle of his arms and she'd closed her eyes for a minute …

And woken up two hours later with a jolt and a gasp, dislodging his arm from around her waist in the process.

She'd waited for him to wake, but he didn't, and, thanking small mercies, she'd slipped from the bed, picked up her nightie and crept from the room. She'd counted the steps to the kitchen and made a warm lemon drink and headed for her favourite sitting room and turned on some music, soft and low, her fingers twitching as she counted her blessings. One-one hundred, two-one hundred, while tears trickled from beneath her lashes at her inability to do something as simple as sleep with the man she loved.

He'd found her there a short time later, his chest bare and his hair a glorious disaster, but he was wearing pyjama pants and carrying the bedspread from his room and a pillow and he tossed them on the sofa before crouching before her and wiping the tears from her cheeks.

He'd left the soft lamplight on and the music playing as he gathered her up and made a nest for them both and then his arms came around her again, her head on his shoulder, her lips to his neck and not an inch between them as he relaxed against her.

"Sleep," he'd said. "I've got you."

It took a while.

It didn't come easy.

But eventually, she slept.

Chapter Nine

TROUBLE CAME IN the form of Max's mother and Carmel's box. Maggie had already received bad news that morning in the form of government refusal to allow her to subdivide Wirra Station. She'd been expecting it, sort of, but also hoping against hope. It would have been so *easy* to continue what she was doing had she been able to sell the land to Max. She'd be debt free, he'd be able to expand his sheep operations, happiness would rain down from the heavens.

But the heavens were having none of it and now they'd have to negotiate grazing rights and she'd have to go to the bank to extend her overdraft in order to pay Max the money he'd already spent and today was not the day to be thinking about any of that.

And now Max's mother was sitting at her kitchen table again and there was something about the way she handled Carmel's box of papers that set Maggie on edge. "Mrs O'Connor, would you like some coffee?"

"I wouldn't say no."

The older woman looked unaccountably nervous. Not a good sign from the reliably unflappable Eleanor. "All set for the ball?"

"Almost. Thank you for accepting the invitation and allowing me to experiment on you."

Eleanor smiled wryly. "Everyone's looking forward to it. Wirralong needs young people with vision and determination. People like my son. People like you. Carmel always said you had no love for this land, but I can see that's not true. No-one could restore it the way you have, and photograph it the way you do, without having a great deal of love and respect for your heritage."

"Thank you." A compliment to remember. "You've seen my pictures?"

"On your blog. It's quite a hit with the locals."

"Oh. Yeah. The blog." She'd started it as a form of outreach to show people what she was up to and it had morphed into a diary of sorts. She should be pleased it was a success. No need to feel so exposed. Outreach. Social skills. She was going to need both if her business was to become a success, and with that in mind she'd even taken Max's advice and loaded up the picture of her scowling at him, caption and all. She'd followed it with an utterly gorgeous picture of him, taken one morning as he'd set the coffee maker to rumbling. She'd weathered the ribald remarks and scolding for scowling at a clearly beloved Max with smiling calm. "I'm not always sure what to put on the blog, but it seems to be working out all right."

"I'm surprised my son doesn't feature in it more. He's over here a lot."

"Yes, well. I'm not sure Max wants to feature on it a lot. He's been on it once."

"I know." Eleanor's voice was dry, very dry.

Maggie served the coffee with biscotti and sat down at the table with Max's mother, because it was the polite thing to do. Wasn't as if she needed to open the box before the ball. It had waited this long. It could hardly house anything that required her urgent attention. But Max's mother kept glancing at it, which meant Maggie kept glancing at it too. Curiosity and dread did not sit well together. "Do *you* know what kind of papers and letters are in the box?"

Eleanor nodded. "I know the crux of it."

"Why do I get the feeling I'm not going to like it?"

"Instinct. Yours is pretty good."

So not helping.

Eleanor still hadn't touched her coffee. "I hope you won't pass judgement. Things are very different now to what they were when your great-aunt was a young woman."

"I wasn't going to open it just yet."

"Then remember what I said when you do."

That could have been the end of it—at least for a while. Maggie had a ball to prepare for and no-one would blame her if she set the box aside for a few days. She couldn't *afford* for Carmel to reach out and mess with her from the grave.

Of course, neither could she afford to obsess over the damned box for days before she opened it.

"Aw, hell." She reached for the box and lifted the lid and the first thing she saw was some kind of clothing wrapped in white tissue paper. She pushed the paper aside and lifted a scrap of ivory fabric out of the box, and it wasn't just any old scrap of fabric, it was a christening gown for a baby, and there was a bonnet, and booties, and she knew where this story was going now but she didn't know the end. The next thing to come out of the box was a birth certificate in an old photo frame. Mother: Carmel Walker. Father: unknown. The baby's name was Joy Lewellyn Walker and she'd been born on Wirra Station. Maggie bit her lip and blinked back tears. "Did she live? Did Carmel's baby live?"

"Yes. The baby's father was a man named Frank Lewellyn. He was Carmel's fiancé and he died shortly after they became engaged. Carmel's father insisted she keep the pregnancy a secret and give the child up for adoption. He handled all the details."

"I see." Maggie felt heartsick for the pain Carmel must have felt. "Is that what Carmel wanted?"

The older woman shrugged an elegant shoulder. "You tell me. Carmel stayed isolated and practically friendless out here on the farm for the rest of her life and when you came along she didn't see it as a second chance, the way some people might. I think she thought she didn't deserve you. Or maybe you reminded her of her failures and she didn't want to keep you close. I'm no psychologist. But there was a lot going on behind the way Carmel cared for you, or didn't care for you, and none of it was *because* of you. I wanted to say that to you so many times."

"But you didn't."

Max's mother suddenly looked older than her years. "I know."

Anyway. Moving on. "Did Carmel ever try and find the baby afterwards?"

"I don't know. Maybe the rest of the letters in the box will answer any questions you might have."

"Have you not read them?"

"Never. But I've thought about the ramifications of Carmel having a child out there somewhere a lot over these past few months. This property is held in trust, yes? And you're the trustee?"

Maggie nodded.

"And were you nominated by name to be the trustee?"

"I think so."

"Check the wording of the will. If control of the trust was to be shared equally between remaining family members, you might have a problem. If you were named as sole trustee, that's the end of it. The company is yours, to do with as you see fit. Carmel's daughter might be able to claim the right to some of Carmel's personal assets but she won't be able to touch the company."

"Check the wording of the Will. Got it."

"And then I suggest you sleep on it a while."

Sleep? Ha!

The older woman must have seen something in her face. "Are you not sleeping well?"

"I sometimes have an adversarial relationship with sleep."

"That doesn't sound good. Does sleeping with my son

help?"

Maggie ran a hand over her face. "Just bury me now. I wouldn't mind. Truly." And then she remembered that Max already half suspected she had a death wish. "I didn't mean that. I was attempting humour and failing, failing badly. Thank you for the box, by the way, but I really need to go and have a minor mental breakdown now. Kidding!" Possibly not kidding. "It's just ... I sold my parents' house on Monday, well below market price, and I heard back from the authorities this morning and I'm not allowed to subdivide the property and sell the grazing land to Max, and now I owe him for all the work he's done on the place and I'll have to tell him, of course, and if I don't have the land he'll have no reason to be with me and I might not control what happens to Wirra Station anyway if the wording doesn't name me and why *would* it name me—"

"*Breathe*, Margaret Mary. My word, you're highly strung. There is no need to panic."

"There isn't?"

A glass of water got shoved in front of her chest. "Take small sips."

Maggie obeyed, while Eleanor O'Connor re-packed the box and put the lid on and pushed it aside and then fixed her with a stern glare. "I'm going to ignore the insult to my son in favour of telling you that his involvement with you has never been about money, or land, or business mergers or status. He cares for *you* and I want you to remember that when you're busy not sleeping. Now, go and get that will.

Let's take a look at it."

Five minutes later, Maggie leaned back in her chair and passed the document across the table to Eleanor. "You know, I could have walked away from this place when Carmel first died. I'd never been happy here. I rarely felt welcome here. But Max said stay a while, it might be different now, and it was, *it is*. I've put my own money into it, mixed it all up because I was the last of the Walkers, there was no-one else left. But that box says there is and the legalese says that Carmel's daughter and her descendants can command equal control of the company, and can I panic now? Because I'm really starting to think this place might not be mine. And that's panic inducing. Trust me!"

Max's mother took a deep breath. "You've only just begun to plough your own money into the company. Your lawyers will be able to annex that for you and if there's a reckoning you'll get it back. You've acted in good faith all along. And who's to say this daughter of Carmel's will ever be found? Or want anything to do with you if she is found?"

"Oh, come on. Sell this place, split the proceeds and they'd walk away with ten million dollars. For showing up!"

"Water," said Eleanor sternly, and Maggie picked up her glass and sipped.

"I've sold things these past months," she muttered in between sips. "Family heirlooms, bric-a-brac, furniture, pictures. And you let me. You knew what was in the box and you never said a word."

"I acted under written, solicitor-witnessed instruction

and you acted in good faith."

"Why would she do that? Why leave this mess for me to clean up?"

"I suspect the situation has always been beyond Carmel's control," the older woman said quietly. "I think she just wanted to bury that bit of her past deep in the ground and never let it see daylight again. She couldn't handle it, not without breaking, so she left it for someone else to deal with. That someone being you. What other choice did she have?"

Maggie closed her eyes and pushed down her panic.

"You can handle this," the older woman said quietly.

"Right." Nothing wrong with a bit of positive thinking. "Yes. Yes, I can." Maggie opened her eyes and reached for the box again. The lid came off, the baby clothes and birth certificate got set aside and she reached in and grabbed a handful of letters and sat them in front of Max's mother. Eleanor O'Connor was a part of this now. "Will you help me skim through these? Please?"

The older woman nodded.

There were love letters from Frank Lewellyn and plenty of them. Maggie left most of them unread but there was no denying that Carmel had been loved by him and loved well. In between Frank's letters they found the occasional clothing receipt.

"This was that yellow gown you wore to your end of school formal," Eleanor said of one of the receipts. "I remember Carmel obsessing over it. It had to be just so. The right colour, the right cut, even the shoes had to be chosen to accentuate the gown."

Maggie frowned. "But Carmel said that that was a discard from a runway show she attended. She knew the designer so she asked for it because it was about my size and she thought the colour would look good on me."

Eleanor snorted. "I hate to break it to you, child, but the House of Dior doesn't generally make clothes that small unless they're making to order. Your aunt called on people from her modelling days to wangle her an appointment with one of their senior designers. She sent measurements and photographs and they created a dress you would feel good in."

And she had felt good in it. For the first time in her young life, Maggie had slid that dress on over her head and looked in the mirror and saw potential.

"And here's the receipt for your earrings," Eleanor said. "They were pretty."

"But those were my mother's. Carmel told me they were!"

"Yes, well. Carmel had a complicated relationship with truth. She thought you would have wanted them to come from your mother. And here's a picture of you. Okay, I'm going to make a *pertaining to you* pile in the middle here." Max's mother dug into the box for another handful of letters and then looked over at Maggie's pile. "What have you got there?"

"You're trying to distract me. Why would Carmel do something like that for me without *telling* me?"

"Eyes on the prize, Margaret Mary—no detours. What we need to know is whether Carmel ever did try and find her daughter, and, if she did, what happened there."

"I can see where Max gets his business acumen from. He seems to have the diluted version. It's quite terrifying."

"Not when I'm on your side it's not, and believe me I am. I've carried this secret around quite long enough. Now sort."

They sorted papers in silence and then Eleanor passed her a letter dated the third of August 1956. The letterhead indicated that it had been sent by an Honourable Solicitor Someone with a London address and it stated that their client had no wish to pursue a relationship with their biological parent, Carmel Walker, and that they trusted this matter was now closed.

"Sounds promising," said Eleanor. "Keep sorting."

Maggie was the one to find the next important letter.

It had the same solicitor's letterhead and informed of Joy Lewellyn Greyson's death. She was survived by a daughter. The letter went on to say that Joy had been a beloved wife, a wonderful mother and a kind and loving person and would be sadly missed by all who knew her. Whoever had written the letter also went on to say that she hoped this sad news and the accompanying photo would help Carmel find closure and comfort in knowing that her daughter had lived a happy and fulfilling life. And then the final line.

Under no circumstances was this letter to be construed as a wish for any further contact.

Maggie could only glance at the photo briefly before tearing up. She'd look at it later. Or maybe she wouldn't.

There were no other letters from the solicitors or from anyone else related to Joy Lewellyn Greyson.

Eleanor sat back with troubled eyes. "Seems clear enough to me. They're not interested."

"And yet someone had the grace, if you can call it grace, to inform Carmel of her daughter's death. Isn't it up to me to do the same? And enclose a copy of Carmel's will?"

"You could do that, yes. Or you could leave it be. It seems to me that in choosing to accept Wirra Station as your home, Carmel has deliberately left that decision up to you."

"I don't know what to do."

Max's mother smiled wryly. "In my admittedly non-lawyerlike opinion, these people would have quite a fight on their hands if they chose to come forward as beneficiaries of Carmel's will or trustees for Wirra Station. Not to say they wouldn't, but they certainly won't be waltzing in to automatically claim what they think is theirs. They're going to need lawyers to prove the connection." Max's mother tapped the two letters. "And very good lawyers if they intend to try and prove entitlement."

A fight. Just what she needed.

"Why don't you go and make us another cup of that exceptional coffee while I finish up here?" Eleanor waved her hand towards the remaining few papers in the box. "It's a shame Max is away. You could have used him as a sounding board."

"I'm pretty sure Max has better things to worry about."

"He likes to help."

"I was really hoping that for once in my life I might be able to help him. Find a way for him to buy the land and me to keep the homestead. Do business together for years to come, given that our goals aren't competing ones. They're quite complementary. That's what I wanted to be able to offer him. Not this *mess*."

Her inability to conceive naturally. Her inability to sleep with him. The possibility of a long, drawn-out court battle over who controlled a parcel of historic Australian grazing land. "No-one would blame him if he backs away once he finds out about this. Even *I* wouldn't blame him." Men had walked away from her for far less.

"You don't have a very high opinion of yourself, do you?"

"I come with problems. All sorts of problems." Maggie looked back over her shoulder at the older woman. "There comes a time when even saviours have to think about saving themselves."

"Frankly, I blame Carmel for your low self-esteem issues. Children aren't meant to be ignored."

"Yes, well. Damage done and all that. I'm rebuilding, and I'm not about to base everything I have here on a lie. Honesty is important to me. I want to treat people how I want to be treated." Maggie nodded to herself. "I'm going to send that London lawyer a letter saying that Carmel is dead and enclose a copy of her will. What happens after that will happen and I'll deal with it."

"Are you sure you don't want to sleep on it?"

"It won't help."

"Oh, that's right. You don't sleep."

She didn't. Not well, not for days. Tears prickled behind her eyes and she set her shoulders and refused to turn around and face the older woman. "Thank you for staying to help sort the letters." Her voice was tight and thready. "You can go now."

And then an arm came around her shoulders and she was being pulled into a sideways hug that had as much awkwardness in it as comfort. "Whatever happens, it will be okay," the other woman said softly. "That last letter had a kindness to it, and if you have to share this place then you will. There are worse things in life than welcoming new family members into it. At least you won't be alone. You'll have family."

But Maggie's experience of family was not the same as other people's. Sometimes family cut down more than they built. "Yeah."

"I don't mean to overstep, but would it be all right by you if I tell Max what happened here today? I'd like to come clean about my involvement in this. It's been a hard secret to keep."

"Of course you should. Just … let me know when you've spoken to him, and then I will. He may not even want to continue with Plan B, which was the long land lease if I couldn't sell the land to him outright. There's a lot to think about. He may need to re-evaluate."

"You really do think he's going to walk away from you."

"No, I—"

Yes.

Anyway. "Do you even want this coffee I'm making?" She pulled out of the other woman's loose embrace. "Because if I have any more I'm going to jitter my way through the day and I'd rather stay vaguely functional. I still have a seating plan to arrange for this charity dinner and I don't know half the people who are coming or who to seat where."

"Give it to me."

Maggie's laptop was sitting on the counter. She opened it up and pulled up the spreadsheet and the pitiful start she'd made on the seating arrangement. All the names were listed in two neat rows of fifty. Anyone with the same last name was seated together.

Maggie slid the computer in front of Eleanor with what was probably unseemly haste. "Next time I'm going to ask people who they'd like to be seated with."

"You know what I think we really need?"

"What?" More to the point, could she provide it?

"Lunch. And then you can put me to work on anything else that needs doing around here and we'll get it done."

Be open and accepting. Be *grateful*. "My dinner waitstaff are turning up in half an hour for a two-hour training run. Not all of them have waited tables before. I was thinking I'd get them to set the main table from scratch and then bring them in here and show them where the catering stations will be and where to collect the meals from and where to return the empty plates. I have the chef's run sheet here so I can tell them what to expect. They need to know how to take the meals out, and serve wine, and how to address meal complaints. I have a list." She leaned over the other woman's shoulder and pulled up a new file.

Eleanor O'Connor skimmed through it. "Do you have other things to do?"

"I have a million other things to do, but none as important. I know the standard of service I want to provide, but I have never in my life led a catering team."

"Fortunately for you, I can help you there."

By the time Max's mother left her to it, Maggie's list of things to do before the ball had been whittled down to last-minute jobs that could only be undertaken on the day of the event—and even those had been allocated to particular people. Bob would cut the flowers *and* arrange them into the vases and bring them in and place them on the tables, because in Eleanor's opinion a gardener should never be denied the opportunity to present their work in the purest light possible and that meant taking ownership of it. He would be aided in this by Carmel's old housekeeper and they would flank Maggie in seats of honour at the head of the table during the meal.

Maggie's two new housekeepers, the sisters who Max had recommended, would lead the waitstaff, allowing Maggie the freedom to mingle and welcome guests. Two of Max's farmhands were now on loan to string fairy lights along walkways, put up parking signs and rake the paths. They would also set up the cloakroom and bring chairs over from the woolshed and stack them on the south-side verandah so they could be easily set out once the dinner was over and the one hundred and fifty-seven additional guests began arriving for the dancing part of the evening.

It had been a masterclass in delegation and household management and Maggie had been more than grateful for the lesson. She'd sent Eleanor O'Connor home with a dozen bottles of wine from the cellar and the warning that less than half of them would prove drinkable. She'd thanked her and meant it, and wondered if this was what maternal support felt like. Bad medicine with good. A little bit bossy, a little bit impatient. One hundred and fifty per cent understanding.

"You're strong, stronger than you know." Max's mother's words echoed in her ear, long after the woman had left. "You've got this."

Chapter Ten

THE DAY OF the ball dawned warm and clear and by mid-morning there was nothing left for Maggie to do but wait. Izzy arrived, and Maggie pounced on her with relief. They had to catch-up on news and catch-up took time. Then she had to hover and fuss and make Izzy look at all the available bedrooms before choosing one, and then make sure she was comfortably settled. There was a fair chance that she'd overdone the hospitality, but Izzy was her first proper guest, and Maggie had a manic amount of show and tell to get through.

The best friend distraction lasted until Izzy had protested that the rest of the tour would have to wait until after she'd had a shower and unpacked and caught her breath, and could manic Maggie please take a break and *breathe*, for just a moment.

"I'm acting mad, aren't I?" she'd asked, and Izzy had laughed and pulled her into a hug.

"A little. Give me an hour and I'll happily join in."

But an hour later Maggie found herself in Max's room— a room she could no longer walk into without conjuring images of him naked and wanting, or playful and teasing, sometimes demanding, occasionally unashamedly begging for her touch. He'd never held back and she'd loved him all the more for it, and she needed those memories to get her through the night.

Surely that kind of behaviour couldn't be faked?

She'd tried calling him after Eleanor had mentioned that she'd been in touch with him, but the call had gone to voicemail.

He hadn't called back and she'd chalked it up to different time zones, but it had been over thirty hours since she'd put that call through and he *still* hadn't called back.

Why hadn't he called back?

So here she was, standing in his room and trying not to think that he'd probably come to his senses during his time away from her. Especially now, with the grey cloud looming over her inheritance. Why *would* he call when he could be gallivanting with Italian fashion models? Buxom-hipped, cat-eyed, clearly fertile Sophia Loren lookalikes. She could picture them. They were everywhere! What on earth could he want with a brown-eyed, mousy-haired, short, slight and overwhelmingly insecure Walker woman? When he could have Sophia Loren!

"Is there any particular reason you're comparing yourself to Sophia Loren, or is this just your idea of fun?"

Izzy leaned against the doorway, her eyes bright and her brown hair tumbling around her face. She'd changed into different casual clothes, but hadn't yet dressed for the ball.

"It's not fun. My meagre curves aren't up to the comparison."

"Few womanly curves are," said Izzy sagely, and this was why she was Maggie's dearest friend. Maggie-the-occasionally-mad did not faze her. Izzy leaned further into the room. "Is this your room?"

"No."

"Didn't think so. Why are you standing in it talking to yourself?"

"I truly don't know."

She herded her friend from Max's room and into her own and gestured towards the two dresses hanging from a garment rack.

"Oh, wow," said Izzy. "Why have I never seen these before?"

"Mainly because one of them was in storage here and the other one I got the other day. What do you think? The red or the yellow?"

"Hold them up to you."

Maggie obeyed. "The red one is me attempting to channel Sophia Loren, but I'm not sure I can pull it off."

"And the yellow one?"

"Has history. It was my high school formal dress."

Izzy looked ever so slightly dumbfounded. "You wore that in year twelve? I bet you slayed the competition. Does it still fit?"

"Unfortunately, yes. No more curves have been forthcoming."

"Wear the yellow one."

"But the red one is nice." Maggie jiggled it on its hanger.

"I'm very nice too."

"Maggie." Uh, oh. It was the please-see-reason voice. Izzy had occasionally used it on her when talking about Richard. "There is no comparison. The red one is off the rack. The yellow one is vintage wondrousness and I don't know where you got it from but you need more of them."

"That obvious, huh?"

"You want to exude class, elegance and effortless sophistication?"

She did. She really did.

"Wear the yellow dress."

By the time Elsa and Serenity rocked up to do hair and nails, already dressed for the evening, Maggie was beyond small talk and heading directly for terror. She managed introductions and luckily the other ladies took it from there.

"Is this Madonna-like calm you've got going the theme for the evening or are you secretly hyperventilating?" asked Serenity, as she stroked colour on Maggie's nails.

Maggie grabbed her hand and held it to her heart, just to hear Serenity laugh.

"Right. Impending heart attack it is. Get your hand back here. You're messing up all my good work."

"Would you like to stay the night?" Maggie asked her and Elsa both. "I have rooms. I have many rooms. And wine. Way too much wine. I shopped at the local vineyards the other day and by the time I got home I swear the wine in the back of the ute was worth more than the ute itself."

"Was it an old ute?" asked Serenity.

"Don't mess with my story. I have wine and bedrooms and a gnawing need for company."

"I could stand to stay over," Elsa said. "Serenity?"

Serenity nodded. "Gotta get in before the paying crowd come knocking."

So that was two more and a potential slumber party in the works. Maggie wondered just how full she'd have to cram the house before she stopped missing Max. "It'll be fun."

And then it was time for Maggie to put on the yellow gown and the strappy stilettoes that went with it and the earrings that did not belong to her mother. She wanted to wear them. It was her way of honouring Carmel. A tribute to the woman who'd raised her from twelve years old onwards.

She pinned an antique flower brooch to the gown, and watched it glitter with the light of real diamonds. She stepped out onto the verandah, intent on entering the ballroom from the same direction the guests would be entering, and then took a detour into the garden at the last minute.

The garden glowed softly beneath the burn of the late summer sun, and she picked three fragrant tips of rosemary and wove them through the brooch for remembrance. Her father, her mother and Carmel. Her family.

Her mother hadn't even had that. Orphaned as a baby, she'd run the gamut of foster homes until she'd come of age. How she'd met and married Maggie's father was a mystery that remained unsolved. There'd been tension because of their obvious status difference. Maggie did remember that.

No romance was perfect.

She came into the ballroom from the middle set of French doors and stood there and took a deep breath because she needed this moment alone. The long wooden table ran the far length of the room and she'd chosen not to dress it with tablecloths. Stainless steel cutlery, white plates, white napkins and gleaming glassware vied for table space with burnished pewter candelabras, white candles and the flowers Bob had collected and arranged. Delicate grevilleas and pink flowering gums, gumnuts, paperbark and tiny wax flowers, and it was beautiful and perfect and her vision to claim.

This was her doing. Her choices and no-one else's had brought her to this moment and she took the time to savour it.

She'd thought she might find it hard to mingle and make small talk as her dinner guests began to arrive, but in truth it was easy. People *wanted* to talk about their memories of Wirra Station back in its glory days. People were *happy* to be invited into her home, and then the champagne started flowing and the finger food began to circulate, and the wine and beer as well, and by the time the meal was served the pre-lubrication had done its job.

The table service was good rather than excellent. Maggie had underestimated the casual familiarity between guests and those serving them. It was easy for her drinks staff in particular to get caught up in conversation with their parents or their grandparents or even their neighbours. Something to work on or maybe even encourage on a case-by-case basis. The food was excellent. The vintage bottles of wine brought out with the main meal—a tasting sensation for the brave—was a nice touch. People liked being made to feel special. It really was that simple.

When the time came for the welcome speech and thankyous, she made them with her heart wide open.

She could do this. Strive to belong, and it was all she could do.

The rest was up to the people.

The dinner was cleared away. More guests arrived and the quintet that doubled as a rock band started their first set. The music was good and as couples began to take to the floor, Maggie couldn't help but search the crowd for a face she knew she wouldn't find. She would have liked Max to be here tonight, if only for the memories she could keep when he walked away. The good dreams rather than the bad.

Max's parents were heading her way and for the first time that evening she had to fight to hold her smile and not flee. Eleanor O'Connor had been good to her. This was the family she might have chosen to have and to hold had she been enough to hold Max's attention.

But she was who she was.

"Congratulations." Max's mother was the first to break the silence. "People are having a wonderful time."

"I hope so."

"Although some of servers seem to have forgotten they're

here to serve."

"I know." Fact was, there wasn't a lot for them to do now that the meal had been cleared away. Not all of her waitstaff were able to serve drinks and she'd deliberately overstaffed the event to begin with.

"You need to step in and make them work, even if it's busy work. Put them to hand-drying the cutlery," the older woman advised. "Do it now. Praise them for their earlier work but be firm."

"I'll do that." Maggie knew an escape route when she saw it. "Enjoy the dancing. The waltz music only lasts for half this set. After that they're switching to bluegrass. Or was it country and western?"

She rounded up the waitstaff stragglers and accompanied them to the freshly redesigned commercial kitchen. Max's mother was right. She needed to give praise and reorganise duties and laugh with the people who'd banded together to work for her. She didn't mind retreating to the kitchen with them. In some ways it was easier being behind the scenes than in the limelight.

Back here she didn't feel quite so alone.

She stayed until Izzy came and dragged her back to the ball. She introduced herself to anyone who stood still long enough. She shook hands, listened to tall stories and told a few of her own. Someone put a glass of champagne in her hand (Elsa's doing) and then another (never let it be said that Elsa and Serenity weren't in cahoots) and then they dragged her onto the dance floor and maybe she didn't need a partner for this part of the evening after all.

If she didn't think about it too much.

She twirled. She laughed. And when the crowd parted and she saw Max standing just inside the door, resplendent in black tie and vaguely tamed hair, she thought she was imagining him. And then their eyes locked, and her heart tried to fly to him while the rest of her stayed perfectly still.

Max was here.

Max was *here*.

And he was walking towards her, all coiled energy and rampant masculine beauty and everybody else in the room faded from her sight.

"I thought you were in Italy," she said when he reached her.

"I was."

"You said you had business that would keep you there until the end of next week."

He looked at her as if committing her face to memory. "I rescheduled."

"I'm not allowed to subdivide the land," she said next, because surely that was a conversation to have in a crowded ballroom. Not.

"I heard."

"And I'm not sure Wirra Station belongs to me anymore. Not wholly. Carmel had a daughter."

"I heard that too."

"So. I'm a bit of a mess. A mess who's in a mess, with more mess to come." He smiled crookedly and lit up her world. "Why aren't you running in the opposite direction?"

"Don't you know?"

"I will have difficulty starting a family, I have intimacy issues and my grand plans for financial stability aren't looking all that stable. I may have to leave here, whether I want to or not. Not even a saviour such as yourself could want to deal with that many messes."

He held out his hand to her and when she took it he drew her in and he was warm to the touch and so steady and sure. "Try me."

"Would you like to dance?" she offered. Because that's what people did at balls. They didn't drag a person into a faraway bedroom and peel off their clothes and refuse to let them out of the room for days.

He moved with her and redefined slow dancing. This was sloth dancing and it worked for her. "How was the dinner?"

"Good, I think. I took a leaf from the Maxwell O'Connor school of community engagement and put myself out there. I was doing quite well—okay, reasonably well—as well as could be expected—and then you turned up and now all bets are off, because you're here. You're really here. Why are you here and not there?"

"I came back early because I heard on the grapevine that some small part of you thought I was only interested in you on account of the farming assets you bring to the table. I'm here to reassure some small part of you that this isn't so. I love your messes, and that's because I love you. It really is that simple." She was taller with her stilettos on, but he still had to bend his head in order for his cheek to brush hers. "Margaret Mary Walker, will you marry me? Will you help me build a home with us at the centre of it? It doesn't have to be this home or this land or even this part of the world, if you decide you can't bear to be here. I'm yours if you'll have me."

Oh, *now* there were tears. "I will."

"Here." He proffered the scrap of kerchief fabric from the top pocket of his jacket and she choked out a laugh because as a mopper-upper of tears it was no use at all.

"Here," he said again, and there was a weight to his beautiful bedroom voice that made her tremble. "Have this too."

It was a ring. A canary diamond that glowed softly yellow and went with her dress and slipped on her finger as if made for it.

"I looked at the white but then I saw this and there was sunshine in it and that's what I want for you. For *us*."

"I love it. I love you." She kissed him, soft and sure, and only when the smattering of cheers and applause reached her ears did she realise they had an audience.

The music stopped and the singer with the midnight voice and a violin in her hand stepped up to the microphone. "Greetings, everyone. I do believe we have a newly engaged couple in the audience. I saw the offer and the acceptance with my very own eyes and I'm here to tell you I saw love. So if you'll bear with us we'll swap out some instruments and give them something romantic to dance to."

The bass guitar player immediately belted out the beginning chords to Deep Purple's 'Smoke on the Water' and drew a laugh, but then he put the guitar away and picked up his double bass and indicated his readiness.

Maggie watched from the circle of Max's arms as the singer directed one of the musicians to the keyboard and another to the backup microphone. "You're all going to know this one," she said when they were set. "And there's only one trick to singing it—you've gotta be a believer. This was written by Hugo Peretti, Luigi Creatore and George Weiss and no-one's ever sung it better than the King." She nodded and the piano started up and so too did the drummer—soft, wispy brush beats and Maggie knew this old Elvis classic, everyone did, and it was perfect and fitting, because Maggie never had been able to help falling in love with this man.

They danced.

They'd never danced together before, but they'd worshipped each other from near and far and maybe that counted for something because dancing in Max's arms felt seamless. Others joined in. Max's parents. Older couples. Younger ones too, and at the end of the song, Max swung her up into his arms and carried her from the room to the punctuation of hoots and wolf whistles.

"There they go, folks." The singer was a comedian. "Have a good evening."

MAX WASN'T INTERESTED in working the crowd or catering to the masses. He'd flown halfway around the world because Maggie had been unsure of his intentions and because he'd needed to spell them out to her before anything else mad, bad or out of the box happened. He'd returned because this was where he needed to be.

"Did you *have* to carry me out of there?" Maggie's words were saying one thing but her arms were around his neck and her lips had found the pulse point in his neck. She was sunshine in his arms and a shining joy in his heart and he was never putting her down.

"I absolutely had to." Nothing surer. "You're mine now and I'm yours and everybody on the planet needed to know it."

"There goes your mystique."

"I sacrifice it willingly." She'd been the stray who'd melted his heart and conjured up fierce protectiveness. The teen who'd expected to be kicked rather than loved. The woman who'd somehow found her feet, even after everything the world had thrown at her. He'd been hers for so long. "Which room?"

"Mine." She set her lips to his skin and he had to stop and push her against the wall and claim her mouth the way he'd wanted to since he first saw her dancing all alone in the ballroom. "I have a new sleeping plan that's going to wage war on those pesky nightmares," she said breathlessly when he'd finished recommitting her taste to memory. "It involves going back to that old psychology technique of trying to reimagine the ending of my dream. This time I don't struggle to get free of you when the fire fills my eyes. I just don't. I know you're there and I know you've got me and that you need me just as much as I need you, so I close my eyes and turn around, into your arms, and I feel your warmth and find the beat of your heart and then I open my eyes ...

"... and there you are."

Epilogue

THE FIRST WEDDING to ever take place on the grounds of Wirra Station was a big one. It was a spring wedding, which made Bob the gardener very happy. It was an unusual wedding in that the bride had no bridesmaids and there was no-one there to give the bride away. She gave herself away, willingly and with an open heart, and the bridegroom did the same.

The bride may have been without bridesmaids, but her arrival had been heralded by a procession of classic cars that now lined either side of the gravel driveway that led to the magnificently restored heritage homestead. The bride had emerged from the very last car in the line-up, a 1933 cherry-red Pierce Silver Arrow, rumoured to be the fourth of only five ever made. The bride's ivory gown had been made by an unknown dressmaker, but it was said they had once worked for the House of Dior. It showed.

The ceremony took place in the garden, with the bride's best friend, Isabella Martenson officiating. The wedding reception was held in the homestead ballroom. The meal was amazing. The waitstaff engaging. The beverage selection had the potential to be described with reverence for many years to come. A bush band was setting up in the woolshed for those who felt inclined to kick on.

The guests were a mix of Wirralong locals, Melbournians, Italians and Chinese nationals. An eclectic mix to match the far-flung influence of this particular couple. It was the wedding Wirralong had been waiting for. A merging of two forward-thinking farming dynasties. It was the creation of family.

Maggie just couldn't stop smiling.

There were last-minute glitches, of course. There always were. Guests with food intolerances they'd forgotten to mention when RSVPing. Lost spectacles, later found on a garden seat. Gate crashers, although few were as boldly, openly out of place as the blonde woman in the blush-pink outfit and the cat-eye sunglasses. She stood at the edge of the crowd, making no move to mingle, and she seemed quite taken with the homestead.

Maybe she was someone's plus-one, arriving late. Either way, she seemed to be on the verge of turning tail and leaving. She watched Maggie approach with something that looked a lot like trepidation.

"Hi." Maggie was learning that when meeting new people it was best to start with the basics. "I'm Maggie, or Margaret if you'd prefer, and you look a little lost." Turning up halfway through a wedding could do that to a person. "There's plenty of food left over if you're hungry."

"I'm afraid I'm in the wrong place." The young woman's accent was pure English—the upper crusty part—and although she may not have been expecting a wedding, her demure day dress, contrasting shoes and clutch, and immaculate presentation could have graced a royal wedding and not been out of place. She was dressed to impress, and possibly to intimidate, but Maggie had just married the love of her life in front of five hundred people and nothing could harsh her buzz. "Or perhaps I'm in the right place at the wrong time," the woman continued. "This *is* Wirra Station. Correct?"

"Yes. And this is the homestead."

"So I'm in the right place. Just the wrong time."

"We're fresh out of rooms, but you're welcome to stay for a while. I'm sure no-one will mind."

The sunglasses came off and Maggie was met with an arctic-blue gaze. "You're Margaret Walker?"

She was young, whoever she was, but she didn't lack confidence. Sharp cheekbones and icy-blue eyes. A wide pillow-crush of a mouth that was just a little bit too big for her face. "Margaret Walker-O'Connor, actually. As of three, no, four hours ago."

"Congratulations." The young woman smiled briefly. "I've no need to interrupt your wedding day. I'll return another time." She turned and there was something about the way she did it, all long-legged grace and coiled energy that tugged at Maggie's memory.

"Wait!" The woman turned her head and there it was again. The echo of a memory she couldn't quite find. "What's your name?"

"Are you sure you want to do this now?"

"It's just a name."

"When it comes to my family the first thing you need to know is that it's never just a name."

She seemed too young to be that cynical. Maggie shrugged. "I don't take much notice of names."

"Obviously. Hyphenating Walker-O'Connor. What were you *thinking?*"

Maggie laughed. For some reason she liked this oddly outspoken stranger. And then the strange young woman seemed to straighten even more. And her posture had been extremely regal to begin with.

"My name is Emmaline Lewellyn Greyson. My mother's name was Joy, and it's my understanding she was born here."

Oh.

Maggie felt the blood leave her face.

"I knew I should have lied about who I was. There is a time for lies and this was one of them." The woman, Emmaline, ducked her head and fumbled to open her clutch. "Here. Don't look so white. I was sent by my family to give you this." She held out an envelope. "It's nothing bad. At least, *I* think it's nothing bad. An invitation for you and your ... husband, is that him over there?"

Maggie nodded.

"Oh, well done! As I was saying, this is an invitation to visit the family pile. There's also some legalese in there about asserting no claim on what's yours. Where's the nearest store? I feel like I should have brought a gift."

Maggie blinked and opened her mouth to speak, but didn't know which parts of the conversation to address first. "The nearest store is about a hundred and fifty kilometres that way. You should forget about gift hunting. The nearest bar on the other hand is about fifty metres that way. I'm heading there now in the hope that a stiff drink will make my white face go away. You could come with me. I have to warn you though, stay away from anyone with a hat and polished cowboy boots on. I will not be made responsible for your downfall."

Emmaline smiled and her slightly regal features transformed into gamine beauty. "A disclaimer! How quaint. And thank you for the offer of hospitality, but I really will come back another time when there are less guests and …" She swiped at the air in front of her face. "… flies."

Maggie laughed but it petered into nothing as she stared down at the envelope in her hands. "Are you sure you're not interested in the assets here? Carmel's personal belongings? You haven't even seen them. Not that I'm not taking care of them, because I am." Obviously. "This is my home."

"And it's a lovely one, but I'll say it again. My family has no interest in your inheritance. The first thing you need to know about us is that we're ridiculously well set."

"You're going to have to explain what that means."

"Meaning we tend to all have titles, status and rather a lot of money. You'll also find we've been proactive when it comes to protecting our own assets from unwanted claims. Each to their own is a splendid way of looking at it. But we would like to extend the limpid hand of kinship to you in typically austere and painfully aristocratic fashion. Which is why I'm here."

"Right," Maggie said faintly. "Thank you."

"It was nothing, my pleasure. I had to get out of England for a while anyway. Too many misogynists and not nearly enough champagne."

"We have champagne." Good champagne, although whether it was good enough for this odd young woman was open to question. "At the bar in the garden and the other bar in the ballroom and then later over at the woolshed, where there'll also be music. You missed the ceremony, the food *and* the speeches and we're heading into the rowdy entertainment part of the evening and you are very welcome to stay. You could compare and contrast the misogyny. Research."

"Maybe one glass of champagne," said Emmaline regally. "A toast to your happiness. It would be the polite thing to do."

"'It would."

"Which way were the cowboy boots again?"

"This way." Maggie started walking. "Never underestimate the appeal of an innocent-looking cowboy on their almost best behaviour. I'm telling you this out of kinship and a vague sense of concern, although I'm not sure if it's you I should be concerned about or them."

"But don't you have sheep? Wouldn't that make them shepherds rather than cowboys? No valiant steeds and moments of man versus beast for these soft fellows, surely. Don't they have shepherd's crooks?"

"Definitely more concerned for you, if that's the approach you're going to be using. Watch out for water troughs, because you might end up in one, and if you see a brown snake, or a black snake with a red belly, or even a tiger snake, call one of the shepherds over and they'll name it for you."

Emmaline shuddered delicately.

"Good luck." Maggie nodded. "You and your ennui will be fine. It'll be fun."

Max waylaid her on her way to the bar, and Emmaline waved her off and kept right on going.

"Who was that?" he murmured as he pressed a kiss to her hair. "You okay?"

"I'm fine. I'm giddy. I'm incandescently happy." She turned her smile on him and watched him warm beneath the heat of it. "And that was Carmel's granddaughter from England."

Max's eyes narrowed. "What does she want?"

"Nothing. Nothing at all." She loved this man, with his keen eye and steadfast support and he loved her right back and made damn sure she knew it. She opened his jacket and slipped the envelope into his inner pocket for safe keeping. "She reminds me of someone."

"Carmel?"

"A little, but she's so out of place and trying so hard not to show it. She reminds me of me when I was younger. I want to make her feel welcome here."

"You will."

Max's unstinting faith in her was like catnip. She wanted

to roll in it and hug it close and never let it go. "I have so much love for you," she told him and watched his smile come out; the one he saved just for her. One smile and a kiss to go with it, and the promise of eternity woven into the fabric of them. "I can't hold it in. I don't know where to put it all." Wicked eyes and the soul of a saviour and he was hers now and she was his. "Any suggestions?"

"I have a few."

"Do tell."

"A kitten," he offered gravely. "I have it on good authority that kittens happily soak up any excess affection lying around."

"I'll consider it. What else?"

"Dogs are good too and they usually come when they're called. Bonus."

"Prepare for a menagerie." She had something to say to him on a topic they'd deliberately kept vague. "How about children? I hear they respond very well to love and safekeeping."

"They do."

"We could aim for one of those."

"If you wanted to." He wanted to, she could see it in his eyes. "We could aim for one of those."

"Or two."

"Or two. I'm in. You know I'm all in when it comes to this, Maggie. Do you really want to?"

With him at her side, nothing was impossible. "I do."

The End

The Outback Bride Series

Book 1: *Maggie's Run* by Kelly Hunter

Book 2: *Belle's Secret* by Victoria Purman

Book 3: *Elsa's Stand* by Cathryn Hein

Book 4: *Holly's Heart* by Fiona McArthur

Available now at your favorite online retailer!

About the Author

Accidently educated in the sciences, **Kelly Hunter** didn't think to start writing romances until she was surrounded by the jungles of Malaysia for a year and didn't have anything to read. Kelly now lives in Australia, surrounded by lush farmland and family. Kelly is a USA Today bestselling author, a three-time RITA finalist and loves writing to the short contemporary romance form.

For more from Kelly:
Visit her website at KellyHunter.co

Thank you for reading

Maggie's Run

If you enjoyed this book, you can find more from all our great authors at TulePublishing.com, or from your favorite online retailer.

Made in the USA
Columbia, SC
22 June 2018